AFRICAN WRITERS SERIES

Editorial Adviser · Chinua Achebe

45

Obi

AFRICAN WRITERS SERIES

OBI

John Munonye

HEINEMANN EDUCATIONAL BOOKS
IBADAN LONDON NAIROBI

Heinemann Educational Books
48 Charles Street, London WIX 8AH
PMB 5205 Ibadan · POB 25080 Nairobi
EDINBURGH MELBOURNE TORONTO
AUCKLAND HONG KONG SINGAPORE

SBN 435 90045 5

Photoset and printed in Malta by
St Paul's Press Ltd

One

JOE GLANCED at his watch. He shrugged. 'Anna ...
Anna ... Anna ...' His voice was low and affectionate.
Each time he called he nudged with his left shoulder.

She stirred and began to stretch.

'Do you know it's three o'clock already?'

'True!' said she vaguely and yawned. 'I've been sleeping.'

The driver broke in: 'Sorry, I wasn't listening. Were you
talking to me?'

'Yes,' he snapped. 'We've been on the road for seven
hours now.'

'Oh, never mind; we'll soon get there.'

'Not if you continue to stop every few minutes.'

'I don't think we'll stop again, but one can never tell,'
said the driver. Then he broke into a song. It was something
about women. He sang loudly, with enthusiasm. When he
came to the refrain his voice swelled, competing with the
engine. 'Indeed a woman excites her husband,' he sang,
'if she allows hair to grow on her chest.'

Anna gave him a hostile, sidelong glance.

She had long decided that there was something evil
about the man, and about the two ruffians that were his
guards. Many things about him gave her this impression:
pock-marked face, snub nose, vulgar speech, sharp eyes,
boisterous laughter, protruding front teeth. And then,
he was very fond of meat. Each time he stopped the lorry,

he would inquire about bush meat or leg of goat; and he would use the opportunity to exchange bawdy jokes with the guards. This was what had forced her to move to the extreme left. She had been sitting in the middle, between Joe and the man. She would rather drink dust, she had pleaded miserably, in a whisper, than continue to sit by the villain's side.

The driver went on singing. To counteract the sound, she began her own song. She sang the Ave Maria. She sang it over and over again. It used to be the most popular song in the convent. They would sing it all day and every day.

It was sixteen years now since she entered the convent, Anna reflected. Mamma had just died. Papa felt he could not bring up the little girl himself; so he sent her to the convent. That was three years before he himself died. People said Papa died of a broken heart, for he loved Mamma very much and could not bear the loss.

The convent was a Literacy Centre and a Marriage Training Home. The white Sisters from Ania had started it. They went back shortly after, leaving the place in the charge of the lay woman they had brought with them.

Her name was Agatha, though most people simply called her Miss. Fat Agatha! Her size was enormous. In true brotherly spirit, the Catholic community of Ossa refrained from making open comments, but not so the rest. They would say: 'Imagine her running a race!' or: 'her buttocks alone are bigger than any house in Ossa!' or: 'No wonder she cannot find a husband. She's two people put together and church men are not allowed to marry more than one; and she wouldn't marry a heathen either.' Agatha knew that the heathens of Ossa said such things about her, but she refused to be ruffled. She was a good-natured and even-tempered woman; and besides, she consigned the idolaters and their tongues to the category of the devil's works, calculated to ruin her mission in the town. In her many years in Ossa, only once was she known to have been seriously upset. That was the day someone suggested, not inaccurately, in her hearing, that she was well over forty-five. She shed tears on that day and some of her pupils wept too, in sympathy.

They all loved Agatha very much, as indeed she loved them. Twice each day—first at midmorning, then at dusk—she would teach them the catechism, or what she preferred to call The Words of Redemption. She would tell them stories about the Creation, the Blessed Trinity, Angels and Saints. She would tell them about the Sacraments, the Ten Commandments with their respective bye-laws, God's Grace, life after death. But more frequently, she would teach them about the Holy Mother who was conceived without sin, and about her only Son who was nailed to the wooden cross because of the sins of men. Each time she talked about the Holy Mother, her voice would descend as if in prayer and she would incline her head to the left and her face would shine with a smile—the smile of faith. They would all listen spellbound. For the stories touched their innermost hearts. Some would exclaim 'Ewu—u!' while others heaved, in compassion or exultation.

The effect was different whenever Agatha talked about Lucifer and the things that belonged to him—hell with all its pains and torments, the fall of our first parents, the deadly sins, false religions, idols, and so on. She would speak about these with horror writ large on her small face. And her pupils would hiss virtuously and wish that Saint Michael would rise and do the thing again. 'Satan often appears in the form of human beings, remember,' was the usual conclusion. Then: 'Kneel down . . . In the name of the Father. . . . Hail Mary. . . .' They would pray for God's Grace to overcome the devil in all its guises.

She taught them to read and write. What her real

qualification was, they did not know and she never discussed it. Speculation had it that she had Government Standard Six Certificate, which was quite a rare qualification those days. There were however several people at Ossa who would not credit that—especially the catechist who himself had failed the examination on two occasions. 'A woman! How could she?' the catechist would sneer. But what made the convent famous was Agatha's proficiency in cooking and dressmaking, and her ability to impart these skills to her pupils. From far and near parents sent their daughters, and men their brides, to be trained there. And more would have been sent but for the three pence charged each month.

She had learnt a lot at the convent, Anna told herself, and by the age of eighteen she was very skilful with her hands. Agatha, who was very proud of her, started to talk about marriage. 'Who is the lucky man that will marry my good daughter?' And not long after, the lucky man turned up.

They were already married before she discovered how the whole thing had come about. It was Father Smith, the then parish priest at Ossa, who had arranged it. Joe was still a mission boy then—and a very popular one. They used to discuss him in the convent, in a rather harmless way. One day she herself said, admiringly: 'He is the only son of his mother, and yet he left her to join the church, and to be a Mission Boy!' And then, only a few hours later, Agatha asked her whether she wouldn't like to marry Joe, the Father's boy who was tall and black and had a long nose and very white teeth.

It was a few months after the wedding that the District Officer at Ossa made Joe the Forest Guard, and sent him all the way to Abagwa. And now, from Abagwa they were returning to Umudiobia, which was Joe's home town.

They were returning to Umudiobia, to live there permanently, and to restore the obi—his father's homestead. That was why he had had to resign.

These were the thoughts that passed through Anna's mind while the lorry bumped and rattled and hissed and squeaked.

*

There was a big jolt. 'Jesus Christ!' exclaimed the driver, gripping the steering wheel firmly. A piece of kola escaped from his hand.

From the back the guards howled.

'It's all right!' he shouted, triumphantly. Then he glanced at the couple on his left.

They were gazing at him malevolently. He tried to placate them: 'I'm sure we're very near to Umudiobia.'

'If you go on driving like that we may never get there at all,' said Joe. But Anna pinched his thigh: she felt it was degrading to quarrel with such a creature.

'But why did you hire a lorry like this?' she interrupted. 'Didn't you know it was so old?'

'Don't forget this is war-time. It's the best that the Transport Control Officer could give us. The better ones are used in transporting timber and palm produce.'

Neither spoke for some time.

'Were you able to see Father yesterday?'

'Yes. In the evening.'

'Good. He was so anxious to see you. I hope there was nothing wrong.'

'Nothing. Just to say farewell.'

'He thinks very much of you, Father does.'

'How did you get to know that?'

'From what he told me.'

'Like?'

'It was when I went to have my new chaplet blessed. He said he would be very happy to hear that we keep up our way of life. "You should be proud that you have a husband like Joseph—somebody who has overcome those temptations to which others in his position have yielded." That was what he told me.'

'He is right,' said he smiling.

'I knew that was what you would say.' Anna laughed.

Not long after, the driver brought the lorry to a stop. He switched off the engine and held on to the brakes. Much of the dust that trailed had disappeared into the bush on both sides of the road, leaving some pinches, as of tobacco snuff, on the outspread leaves. What had survived now caught up with the vehicle, and enveloped the entire body.

The horn sounded three times.

Then from the back, one of the guards leapt down. He had a wedge in his right hand and chewing stick in his mouth. His eyes half closed, he pierced his way through the dust to the offside rear wheel. There he dropped the wedge, and kicked it to until it had jammed the tyre. 'Okido!' he cried, and his jaws began to work on the stick. He was a slouchy little fellow and he bore himself as if irresponsibility was part of his profession. 'Le' go now!'

A fairly large crowd had gathered in the market square which was some two hundred yards further on. They now began to move towards the spot. They saw somebody climb down from the right side of the front seat. He was the driver; they could easily identify him from his careless look. And from the left side a woman came down. She was smiling fondly at everybody. 'Who was she? Perhaps . . .' Then they saw another, a man, coming down, close behind her. 'That was them!' they cried; and they rushed forward and roared with delight.

Two

TOM-TOM BEATS sounded and gun-shots tore the air. Then came Emelumadu's voice. He said:

'A great thing has happened, has happened, has happened; a great thing has happened. . . . This is the cock, the cock, the cock; this is the cock. . . . I'm the cock, Umudiobia, and I've spied the rising sun. . . . Okafo it was who begot him. . . . Okafo, you are not dead; you are only asleep. . . . Umudiobia of ten villages and two, is my voice not to your liking?'

They applauded.

He craned his neck and he cried again. But now he gesticulated too, pointing skyward from time to time, smiling. Without doubt, the thing had gone right into his brain.

Somewhere to the north a cannon began to boom. One . . . two . . . three . . . four. . . . There were twelve of them, one for each of the villages in the town.

The crowd soon numbered many hundreds.

A good number of them, probably up to a fifth, were children. These showed greater interest in the lorry than in the very important personalities that had just arrived in it. From safe distances they admired and mocked at the same time. They admired it for its strength but mocked at its ugly face. They pointed at the rolling feet with which the thing could run faster than any dog. They stared at the two big, unblinking eyes which straddled the face. A few speculated on the round object inside, on top of which the driver rested his hands, and by means of which he could communicate with the four hundred spirits that growled in its heart as it moved, telling the spirits the road and the bends. Those of them that were school children stared at the inscription on its forehead; or they tried to pronounce but soon gave it up as a mistake. 'PSALM,' they spelt; 'and 25 after that!' Probably one of the uncouth guards wrote the nonsense. The most daring ones among them pushed their way through the crowd and touched the vehicle, though with trembling hands. For never before had they seen such an ugly specimen.

Many in the crowd were members of the Roman Catholic Church. They had come to the square as a group to welcome a very important member. They regarded Joe's return as a big score over the other sects. 'Let them produce their own,' their women boasted, referring in particular to the more serious rival, the Anglican Church. For Umudiobia now had three churches, each of which was trying to win a greater part of the town than the others. The Catholic Church was the first to arrive, come from Nade nearly seventeen years back. The Anglican Church arrived next. The Holy Spirituals arrived last. The Spirituals were completely new in the area. However, they had already won a great number of converts. The secret of their success was their music—their clapping and singing and dancing; and besides, they allowed their members to marry as many wives as they could afford. There were also several stories about how, merely by praying, they had made mothers of barren women.

Some just stared at the loads which the guards were now taking down from the lorry. Two big iron beds with heavy posts, as yet in pieces; four trunk boxes (no doubt all filled with money); cupboards, tables, chairs; a big standing mirror; a bicycle; a number of cartons. . . . Could all that belong to just one man and his wife? So that was what white man's work meant! Odiegwu! Nobody in all the places they knew had so much costly property.

'But did they come alone?' someone would ask.

'How?' another would reply.

'Where are their children?'

'Sh—' Then she would whisper: 'I hear they have none yet.'

'Didn't I hear they got married years ago?'

'Don't ask your sister.'

Then there were Joe's closest relatives. They included Chiaku his mother, and Obieke, Adagu and Willie, who were all cousins. They stood closest to him and Anna, protectively; some kept watch over his property. It was they who had arranged for all the loud reception. They had brought the tom-tom and the guns. They too had hired Emelumadu and arranged for the cannon-shots.

Presently one of the guards cried 'Koi!' at the top of his voice to draw attention to himself.

'If any of you here wish to travel to Ikida, or to Ossa, let them pay just sixpence and they will be there before spittle dries on the ground.'

Nobody offered to travel. They rather advised him to keep his jaws busy on the stick in his mouth. He went back and reported to his master.

'Push the lorry then and let's move,' ordered the driver sorrowfully. 'I was almost sure it would be like that.'

The horn sounded. The crowd moved out of the way. The guard removed the wedge. The two of them began to push. They held their lower lips firmly with their teeth, their eyes bulged, and they strained all their muscles.

The lorry jerked. But the engine would not start. They continued to push.

Then there was a deep, explosive sound. The gear had engaged and the engine had been fired into life. Still holding down the clutch, the driver blazed on mercilessly and the over-fed engine returned a terrific roar. Hands now on the tail-board and feet off the ground, the guards remained suspended for a few moments; then they volleyed themselves up, expertly, into the cavern.

A good many of the children—the more athletic ones—made to pursue. But the guards would not allow this—not when there was not a single passenger in the town. With both palms the guards swept a good quantity of sand from the floor of the lorry. They threw it out for the benefit of the children's eyes, shouting:

'May grass overgrow the approach to your father's compounds, you little things.'

*

Attention was at last concentrated on the husband and his wife. With that spontaneity of service which was then a habit among the people, some stalwarts came forward and offered to carry the loads. All they would like to know was where to take the things to, said one, an eager-looking youth. It was Obieke who replied. Obieke felt it was too early yet to allow Joe to speak.

'Why ask? To his father's compound, of course.'

It took another thirty minutes before Joe and Anna could extricate themselves from the delirious crowd. And even then, quite a good number still followed. Among them were the umuada, daughters by direct descent of the extended family which had begun with Udemezue of Burning Eyes, four generations back. The umuada formed themselves into a distinctive group at the rear and made a song on the day's happy event. As they sang they clapped their hands and swayed their bodies.

The soloist said: 'He has come back to his people in a grand style.'

They answered: 'Nobody in the land has done such a thing before.'

'Think of the white man's work he has left to return to his own.'

'Nobody in the land. . . .'

'But tell me, my sisters, who can say that Udemezue was not great?'

'Pure nonsense, that's what such talk would be.'

(Obieke sighed: 'These women and their mouths!')

'Kili Kili Kilio!'

'Yoh!'

'Kilio!'

'Yoh!'

'Kilio!'

'Yoh!'

'Gome!' the gong droned, just once. There was a pause. It droned again. They resumed:

'Have you seen the beautiful one he's brought home for us?'

'Nobody in the land. . . .'

'See her legs and see her face!'

'Nobody in the land. . . .'

'See the grace with which she steps!' Joe caught Anna's eyes and they both began to laugh, and the chorus boasted that nobody in the land had done that either.

'Ojukwu of Umudiobia, only one thing we beg of you.'

'Proceed, Sister, your mouth is good.'

'It's to spare their lives and give them what they need most.'

They yelled and they asked her to keep her mouth moving.

'Give them many many children who will sustain the line.'

There was prolonged applause.

A troupe of folk-musicians were already assembled at what used to be Okafo's compound under a palm-frond shed. As soon as they heard the applause they began to perform. But there was not yet enough spirit in the music. As the saying went, they were just tuning their hearts.

It was when the guests of honour had come in that the musicians rose to their usual height. The clappers, the rattles and the music pot blended faultlessly with Okoye's voice. Okoye was full of saws and proverbs today and he wove them beautifully into the rhythm. And while he sang, his thumbs plucked steadily at the tips of the metal prongs which were set on the big calabash bowl he carried in his hands. Now he would incline his head towards the other members of the troupe, as if he was serenading them; now he would stand erect and still and pour out his heart in that liquid voice for which he was widely known.

Then there was a change in the movement. The song had turned into an epic. Okoye was relating the story of Joe's life, as he had learnt it from the relatives. The clappers and rattles dropped out now, leaving the narrative with a cool dignity. The crowd stood in their places and watched, and whispered their comments. They liked the man's voice very much, but what they liked most was the aptness of his compositions.

Three

THUS DID LIFE return, at long last, to the site of the old compound. Nearly eighteen years had passed since the place was last inhabited. To be exact, it was on the day Joe, then called Nnanna, fled from Umudiobia to Nade with Chiaku his mother. He was only thirteen years and some months old then.

Joe would always remember the exciting incident that led to their hurried departure from Umudiobia. He beat Adagu and Obieke during the day. He beat them so hard that their lips were swollen and they cried and cried. And when Amanze, their father, heard about it in the evening, he summoned Chiaku for questioning. There in Amanze's house, a fight ensued between her and the children's mothers. Joe came in just in time and shot an arrow into Adagu's mother's leg, and thus saved his mother from Amanze and his two wives. The following day, very early in the morning, they fled to Nade—his mother's hometown. They did not return to Umudiobia afterwards; it was from Nade that he later went to Ossa with the priest, to become a Mission Boy.

There was a small house of red-mud walls and thatch roof at the middle of the site, built by Obieke and his Kinsmen. Obieke had visited Abagwa the year before on Joe's invitation. That was when they made arrangements for the building.

'I shall need a house of my own immediately I arrive,' Joe had said. 'Do you think something can be done?'

'Why not?' Obieke had replied, transparently happy. 'There won't be any difficulty about that.'

'I would like it built within the site of the old compound.'

'I follow you.' And then he nodded approvingly. His tone was soft and low, and sincere. He mused: 'The house should be as close to Okafo's grave as possible. Yes, so that the father's spirit will guide and protect the one and only son.'

'How much do you think it will cost?'

'Anything you can afford, Father.' He would often call him Father. Though baptized now, Joe was still their grandfather Okoli come back to life.

Then Joe counted four pounds ten shilling, all in coins, and handed it over to Obieke.

Obieke left for home the following day. He arrived two days later. Then he summoned his Umunna, the kinsmen, and told them the news. They were very pleased to hear that Joe was coming home to restore the obi.

The work was started a few weeks after. They used up for the walls all the heap of red-earth mud which Obieke had had trodden and hurled up for some other purpose. And they sited the building close to the healthy and sturdy palm-tree which was almost at the centre of the old compound. The tree marked Okafo's burial place. They even went further than that: they reclaimed the entire site from bush.

Compared with the house in which Joe had lived at Abagwa with Anna, this was a mere shanty. It had only two small bedrooms and a narrow sitting room. But it satisfied their immediate need. Besides, as the saying went, a man's home is never too mean for him. So Joe thought within himself. He would one day, and that soon, build himself a solid, permanent residence. It would probably be one of the best of its type so far in the area. He had the money for that; it was a question of settling down first.

*

For days and days, and then for weeks, visitors came to welcome him and his wife. Some came in groups; others came singly.

Prominent among the visitors were sons and daughters of the family—that is, all those that were descended from Udemezue of Burning Eyes. These were countless, and yet everyone of them made sure he located himself, to the host's hearing, in the family tree. They came without previous warning, by night as well as by day. Some of them brought jars of wine, which they themselves drank. That was in addition to the food they were given to eat. Joe would also give them some special gifts to take home. For that was the type of reception a great man should expect among his people. A visitor had only to prove that he was a relation, or even a friend of the family, and he could expect some gift as of right.

Twelve men representing the Roman Catholic community in Umudiobia, male section, came at midday one Sunday. They had informed him that they would come to pray for him and his wife. In actual fact, they prayed for less than twenty minutes and were then feasted for over an hour. Then one of them whose name was Jerome rose to say a few words of wisdom for the benefit of the generous host and hostess.

Jerome started by thanking the couple for their magnanimity. It had been a great feast, said, he. 'One could even go so far as to liken it to the kind of treat the Israelites had in the desert.' Then he proceeded to describe Joe's return to Umudiobia as a timely reinforcement in the battle against false faiths. 'We know the size of the battle, for we've been fighting it,' he said. 'I was one of those that started the church in Umudiobia and I am resolved to fight for it till the end of my life.'

'Pillar!' they hailed him. He was the most influential member of the church in Umudiobia. And he was very devoted too. For example, only a week after his conversion, Jerome had, in proof of his sincerity, summarily dismissed four of his five wives, retaining only the first who incidentally was the least beautiful. And his faith had not flagged since then.

He had spoken for about fifteen minutes. Then he concluded:

'We all can see you're a wealthy man, my child. I would advise you, don't allow yourself to be carried away by the things of this world. For nobody can serve God and Mammon. And again, the same Bible says that it's difficult for a rich man to enter God's Kingdom. Just make yourself like one of the little ones in Umudiobia. In the name of the Father. . . .'

They prayed aloud, together. But Joe could not bring himself to join. He could not even pretend that he was praying. He was wondering in his mind. Why had the man spoken like that? Perhaps there was nothing in it.

*

Five weeks had already passed since their return, and the noises and merry-making had begun to die out. Some of the kinsmen gathered outside the house, in the open front yard. They did not come on any specific business. It was just one of those occasions in which one came in and found others and decided he should stay on. The time was mid-morning and the day was a market day. They had a few hours before the market would start. So they sat at ease and conversed.

'My brothers, we did good work here, didn't we?' someone asked.

'How?'

'Look at the roof. It's so nice. And look at the walls.'

'It's very nice,' Joe acknowledged, nodding. 'Do you know, in Abagwa people don't have houses that are half as good as this.'

'True!'

'They live in small huts. . . .'

They had ceased to talk now. They were all listening. That had become their habit. Each time he opened his mouth they would listen and stare. He was an important man; he had gone to places; he had worked for a white man and even lived with a white man.

He wore a white shirt, khaki shorts and brown canvas shoes, while the best-dressed of the rest had a wrapper round his waist and others just tied strips of calico cloth between their thighs. And then, to add to his superior appearance, there was the dialect he spoke. It was soft, slippery and light-tongued. It had an exotic appeal; and besides, it contrasted with the harsh sounds and heavy-lipped speech of Umudiobia and its neighbours. His countenance was serene and he looked distant and reserved. However, he was not as relaxed as they themselves. But how could he be when he was still new to the land? So they would reason among themselves.

'As I said before, I was indeed surprised to see the house when I arrived,' Joe continued after some time. 'And then, the entire site was reclaimed! Believe me, I thought I would wade through bush into the hut.'

They answered now, one after another:

'Spit it off!'

'Such talk does bite the ear.'

'Wade through bush when you've brothers alive?'

'The spirits of our fathers would have strangled us all to death. . . .'

One of them tapped at his snuff-box with the thumb, then opened it. His countenance fell and he hissed mournfully. 'Nothing inside it and yet the weather is so cold!' He hissed again and dropped the box together with its lid disgustedly on the ground.

Joe went into the house. On his return he brought a bottle of gin.

'For the chill.' He raised the bottle up for everybody to see.

The conversation warmed up as they drank. They talked about some of the good things that had been coming into the land, of which gin was definitely one. Gin, said they, had more power over toothache than all the medication of the local doctors.

Then, unannounced and unexpected, Willie, Joe's cousin, came in.

Willie had been away from Umudiobia for the past ten days. Where exactly he had gone to not even his brother, Obieke, could tell. Of late, the Kinsmen had begun to get seriously worried about his movements and, what was worse, about the things that were coming out of his mouth. He was either out of Umudiobia, without their knowledge, or he was telling the townsfolk that the white man must go home and leave black men to rule themselves.

'I'm just back from Ania,' he announced gallantly before they could say anything. Then he grabbed the bottle and poured himself some gin.

'But who sent you there?' someone asked in jest.

He guffawed. He took another sip and smacked his lips luxuriously. 'We are arranging how to fight for your liberation. When we win you'll all be happy.'

They fell on him.

'He comes again with his mouth!'

'You've never wrestled since you were born. How then can you fight?'

'What harm did the white man do to you, brother?'

'This white man you want to go home, is he not the one that made the cloth you wear? Are you going to surrender it to him before he leaves?'

'Go on, answer them,' Joe said, laughing quietly.

Willie merely waved them aside, signifying that they were totally ignorant of the issues involved. And the topic changed.

About ten minutes passed.

'Sh!—'

They subsided.

'Let's listen to the story he's telling us, please.'

All went silent.

'Please start again, from the beginning.'

Joe did. It was the story of his experience at Orola, the land of the Just Oracle.

*

It happened in his first year at Ossa. He went with four others to try to persuade the people of Orola to embrace Christianity. It was the priest that sent them.

Orola was a small town about fifteen miles south-west of Ossa. It had never been great in war and its soil was not fertile. Yet it was known far and wide. That was because of the oracle there which was called the Just. From very distant lands people came to the oracle in quest of justice, and were only too pleased to pay the prescribed fee—even if that meant emptying their barns or treasure vaults—in order to obtain its verdict. And Orola became prosperous from the wealth they brought.

It was to this town that Rev. Father Smith decided he

should bring faith. His first step was to send an advance party to explore the ground. If he had consulted the District Officer at Ossa, he would have learnt that the oracle had a network of eyes all over the area in the form of traders, gypsies and refugees. Father Smith did not know (until it was too late) that the oracle's spies had been watching him since his arrival at Ossa—watching the new thing which might destroy the establishment on which the fame of the town rested.

Many people at Ossa knew why Joe was specially chosen as one of the five that should go to Orola. Father Smith wanted to set him on an adventure that would challenge his energy and strength. Joe had then a reputation for pugnaciousness. In the school they would refer to him as the Father's boy who argued all his points with his fists.

Then one day Joe went to the extent of brandishing his clenched fist before his teacher. In fairness to him, he acted under great provocation. That particular teacher caned harder than any masquerade and had left bruises on Joe's back on two different occasions. However, the news got to the priest through the headmaster, through the teacher. Joe was given six strokes of the cane on the buttocks. 'You could have been a very good lad, and I'm sure you could still be one, if you would only stop this uncivilized be-haviour.' That was what Father Smith said in the end in his deep, kind voice. Then: 'I'll soon find you something that will take up all that energy that bubbles up in you.'

That was barely two weeks before the journey to Orola.

They set out very early in the morning. By noon they were at the outskirts of the town. The narrow, winding path was strewn here and there with sacrificial heaps—woven palm-fronds, chickens, potsheds, cowrie-shells, animal flesh, baskets. The forest was thick on both sides. There was dense silence. Chills ran down their spines, yet they continued.

Something growled. They stood still, puzzled, terrified. Some seconds passed. Something cracked and something whistled past, within a few inches of Joe's right ear.

'What was it?' panted the catechist who led the party.

'It's a gun. Please let's turn back,' said Edward. His face was pale and his voice sounded pathetic and his tall skinny frame seemed to shake. But the catechist merely crossed himself.

Then the shots came in quick succession and from both sides of the forest. The catechist was the first to fall. Edward followed. They were both bleeding, one from the head and the other from the heart; and the blood spurted out. The firing ceased.

The rest lay flat on the ground and began to wonder what to do with the bodies. And then, scores of men came out quietly from the bush. The men proceeded to gag them, after which they blindfolded them with the hard and opaque skin of palm-branch stalk; finally, they tied their hands and led them away.

Two full days must have passed—they were not sure for the fold was still over their eyes. Then they were led out and the fold was removed. It took some time before they could see. They were all exhausted and badly bruised. Before them stood Mr Raymond, the District Officer, with some soldiers.

It was months later that they got to know what had transpired at Ossa between the District Officer and the priest; and then at Orola between that Officer and the high priests of the Oracle. Father Smith had made a report to Raymond when a day had passed and the party was still not back. Having fumed for some time and condemned aloud the reckless sense of adventure in the Irish idealist, Raymond decided in the end to visit Orola with a small force. At Orola he assured the high priests that he had not come to disturb the oracle; that he only wanted the five men back. It would be no use their saying that they knew nothing about the party; he was sure the five were being held captives somewhere. But if they should refuse to listen to words of peace, then it would be his duty to order the soldiers to go ahead. The bluff worked. After a hurried meeting, the priests decided to produce the three. They could not account for the remaining two, they said.

*

Everyone of them exclaimed and some snapped on their left palm with the right fingers when he concluded the story. The news that had reached them in Umudiobia at the time about the incident had been incoherent and even incredible. They had to send two people to Ossa to find out the truth. But then, the excitement was so much that none had bothered about the details when the two returned; they were satisfied to learn that they were alive. This was therefore the first time they were hearing the entire story, and first-hand too.

'That British imperialist, the D.O.!' Willie protested. 'He promised he would not disturb the oracle if the captives were produced, and yet he destroyed the whole place afterwards. Isn't it betrayal of confidence?'

'He destroyed it because they killed the remaining two,' Joe explained.

'Unless that. But why didn't the Father go in person? He purposely sent you people there to get killed. That's the very thing they are doing with our people who are fighting in the war. Man's inhumanity to man,' said he in English, then reverted into vernacular: 'He it was who led those two men to their death!'

'Nobody killed them,' another said. 'It was the oracle which they sought to destroy that took their lives.'

'Nonsense. What happened in the end?' countered the only one among them, apart from Joe and possibly Willie, who was a Christian. 'Didn't the D.O. destroy the oracle? Orola now has a school in its place.'

'You are happy about it, are you? Think about what has been happening in the land since then!'

'That's true,' another joined. 'Everything has changed since then. The soil is no longer fertile, for the earth, outraged, has withheld her kindness from man. People cheat these days—they cheat even their own brothers. Women bully their husbands and produce children that resemble neither father nor mother.'

'And that's exactly why Uzondu has refused to marry,' Uzondu said. They broke into laughter.

'Speaking seriously, count how many cases of robbery alone we've had in this town in the past few moons'.

Anna brought a plate of yam stewed with fish. She placed it on a low stool. Then she went back into the house.

'May we eat what our wife has brought to us,' Obieke said and he took the first piece. While they ate the argument went on.

'Is it surprising then that so many horrible diseases now visit the land?'

'Even animals too have changed their ways. The fowl no longer sleeps in its pen; it prefers tree-tops. That is because the ground has been fouled by men.'

'No, say by the Christians.'

'Yes, by them,' he mumbled, swallowing. 'The cock crows any time it likes. And the dog barks at its owner and bites his children. The goat rejects its fodder; it prefers yams.'

'That's true, Brother. I agree—' He began to cough, violently.

'Somebody give him water, please,' said the Christian, laughing. 'That ought to be a lesson to any of you that may want to say something bad about the church. T-hi t-hi t-hi!

God knew Willie and I couldn't face the six of you so he sent pepper to our aid.'

Willie promptly asked the speaker to count him out. 'I don't belong to your imported religion,' he said. 'I want our own African Church.'

'Their camp is now divided,' Uzondu observed, and then crammed a big piece of yam into his mouth.

'So you people believe it was the oracle of Orola which came all the way to infect the animals in our town?' asked Joe, smiling indulgently.

'In a way, my son,' answered Ikeli, the eldest of them all. 'The gods revolted in sympathy and their wrath has spread far and wide.'

The plate was now empty. Uzondu set about rendering it dry with his fingers. The rest rose and began to leave.

'He did not offend against the gods,' Ikeli pronounced, sagely. 'If he did he would have died on that day.'

'Very true,' they confirmed in a disorderly chorus.

Four

'DID THEY FINISH the bottle of gin?' she asked. It was a few days later and they were alone in the house, for a change. The time was a little before sunset and a cool, gentle breeze was blowing into the sitting room. They sat facing each other. Joe was idle while Anna was busy knitting a woollen pullover for herself.

'They did,' he answered. 'But for Willie they might not have.'

She made a wry face. 'I don't like him.'

'Why? He is a kind man in spite of all that he says about fighting British imperialists.'

'What have they done to him? They it was who brought the clothes he wears, the lorry he takes to Ania, and some-body's gin he drinks like water.'

'You will ask him when next you see him.'

'And then, he goes on to talk nonsense about the priest of God, and the church. Is he not the person who once said that all churches are the same in that they are here to make money which they send home to white man's country?'

'He says terrible things at times.'

'I don't like him,' she affirmed.

'You like Jerome then?'

'Who? The Pillar?'

'Yes.'

She paused. 'That man who talks as if he was Saint Peter that founded the Church?'

He laughed. 'No, he regards the church here as his private property. Others are there by sufferance.'

'I can't understand why he should behave like that. Look at all he said on that day! That man is jealous of you, Joe.'

He grunted mysteriously.

'Willie doesn't go to church any more and you don't like him. Jerome goes regularly and you don't like him either!'

'You are free to like the man. But remember,' said she with a smile, 'he has decided you will not enter the Kingdom of God.'

There was an interval during which she went on knitting while he hummed a song.

'What about Uzondu, do you like him?' he asked.

'The fat one?'

'Yes.'

'Oh, I like him very much. He makes me laugh. I don't know his wife.'

'He has none. He's too easy-going to think about marriage. But he has no ill-feeling in his heart. Yesterday at Obieke's house he kept us laughing until our ribs nearly broke.'

'One very good thing I've noticed in your people is their sense of humour. And on the whole, I think they are nice—the men I mean. I love Obieke best of all. He has the sense of an old man and he is kind and gentle. Only his wife—'

'True, the woman is his bane,' he concurred. 'And what about the umuada, don't you like them too.'

She clucked, then, rather reluctantly: 'They are fair. I like how they received us. I think they are all very fond of you.' She paused. 'Only—' She looked up and caught his eyes.

'What?'

'I don't know.' She smiled, then paused—'Udemezue's daughters!'

He broke into laughter.

'They are very boastful.'

'Why shouldn't they be?' asked he with humour, and with veiled sarcasm. 'After all we are a big family in Umudiobia.'

She nodded cynically.

'Udemezue was the greatest man Umudiobia had in his days. He was even greater than the paramount chief himself. Hundreds of slaves, scores of wives—Don't laugh. He was tall and huge and his eyes were fierce and he frightened people into surrendering their wives and property.'

'Stop!' She was laughing convulsively. When she subsided she wiped the tears from her eyes.

'Is that why they called him Udemezue of Burning Eyes?'

'No other reason. You see then that umuada do not boast in vain. . . . Anna, oh, I forgot to tell you.'

'What?'

'Mother sent word she will be here day after tomorrow. She did not say the exact time.'

'I must start to prepare for her coming,' said she dutifully. 'What will she like to eat?'

'I can't speak for her but I can speak for myself.' He rose. 'I'm hungry.'

When she looked up she did not see him. Instinct born of experience told her he was creating some havoc inside her room. She rose noiselessly and tiptoed into the room. But she was too late. Joe had already discovered the coil of fish covered up in a basin, and he was now putting a sizeable piece into his mouth.

'He-i-i!' She slapped his elbow, ineffectually. 'That's the only fish I have in the house.'

'There's still a lot left.' He sounded like a tired masquerade.

*

Chiaku arrived with her three children at the hour when the tapper was supposed to be completing the morning round of the palms. They had left their house in Nade at the first hint of dawn, as she had been anxious to discuss something rather serious, to her, with Joe before the crowds would start to pour in. Three times now she had visited him since his return; and on each occasion she had found the whole place filled, with the result that she had no chance to talk to her son. Today it must not happen again. She must talk with him.

Chiaku was therefore disappointed when she found a group of people gathered already in the house—even at that hour! Two persons she easily identified. They were Obieke and Uzondu. To Obieke she showed a cold face. She would never forget that bleak evening, many years back, when Obieke's father, Amanze, made her decide to flee Umudiobia. She was better disposed towards Uzondu. In those days, Uzondu was a slow, clumsy lad, good-humoured and friendly; everybody liked him, and every boy of his age threw him in wrestling. She herself too had liked him very much. He used to remind her of her brother Oji, now dead. The others she took for parasites who had come to borrow from her son. And in fact, her guess was not entirely incorrect. One of them, a son of a daughter of the land, was there to raise a loan to enable him pay bride-price on his second wife. As yet, however, he had not been able to get the thing out of his mouth.

Joe came out from the sleeping room. 'Mother!' he exclaimed, stepping towards her.

'My husband's father!' said she in reply and caught hold of his left wrist as if she was afraid he would escape. 'I've forgotten that name you now answer. I know you as Nnanna and nothing else.' Everybody laughed. She dropped his wrist and clasped his forearm. 'Giant!' She looked up at his face. There was a clear six inches between their heads. 'See him, he's growing fat too.' She began to stroke his chest. 'He used to be a tiny string.'

'I thought you had seen him before—I mean since his return,' someone said.

'She wants to make sure that he's complete,' another said.

'You better carry him in your lap and give him breast milk,' said the first speaker.

Joe indicated a seat. She sat down, looking around with a proprietary air. The children stood beside her.

'Obieke, how is your family?' asked she casually.

'Very well. I spoke to you but you were too busy looking after the new-born baby,' Obieke replied.

'You've not asked me about mine,' said Uzondu.

'Is he married now?'

'Yes, his twentieth wife arrived yesterday,' another replied. Then they all joined in taunting Uzondu. In reply he asked them to start looking for a girl, but only such as would be prepared to swear never to cause him any worries.

'Have you greeted your brother?' She pushed the children forward, towards Joe. The biggest said, 'Coomaisa,' and the other two followed suit. Joe shook hands with them one after another.

Joe went into the sleeping room and brought some lumps of sugar. He gave them one lump each, and they threw it into their mouths. 'Hu-u-uh!' they exclaimed and smacked their lips and smiled with pleasure. 'It's very sweet!'

'Eat, my children; it comes from your own brother's hand,' she said. 'Let me have one of those, my husband's father.' She stretched out her palm.

When the sugar had begun to melt in her mouth Chiaku declared that the children had understated the fact. But did the thing have any power over toothache? She was asking because some wicked spirits had been pulling at her teeth for months now. Then, much to her disappointment, Joe replied that sugar did not go with aching teeth. She went outside and there she spat out the sugar. She spat until her mouth was almost dry of saliva.

'But where is the wife you brought home?' asked she sternly when she returned to the house.

'That's true.' He rose. 'She's sleeping; she's not quite well. I'll go and call her.'

'Sleeping still at this hour?' she queried and demanded an explanation. 'Or is it a happy sickness?'

'Who knows?' the rest said.

Anna had been awake most of the time and had been listening to the voices. As soon as Joe came in she rose. There was a brief conspiracy. Then, smiling, she gave a big groan, loud enough for them to hear; and she rubbed her face with some ointment, giving it the bloated appearance often noticed in female patients. Finally she tied her head with a scarf and made sure the edge of the cloth reached her eyebrows. Then she came out to the sitting-room, clumsily, dragging her steps.

She went straight to the corner where Chiaku sat. She knelt down and embraced her. Then she began to inspect the children.

'Mother, this one resembles you' said she as she came to the second, a girl aged about eleven. Her name was Chinwe. 'I had better ask her to stay with me.'

'Just as you like, daughter,' replied Chiaku agreeably. 'But I will need to tell her father first.'

'Hei!' Anna exclaimed shortly after. She had come to the third. 'This is the one who resembles Joe very much.'

'Not when he has such short legs,' Uzondu corrected.

'I mean his complexion. Blacker than iron pot.' She began to rub the child's cheek with her finger. 'Let me see if I can scrape off some of the blackness.'

They all roared with laughter. In the meantime, Anna had forgotten that she was supposed to be ill.

'Mother, come in and see what we brought home,' she said some time after.

'Yes, I will.'

They went into the room. The children followed.

Chiaku stood speechless and gazed at the big iron bed, and at the posts which had brown ornamentation in places. She looked at the trunk boxes. She shrugged and smiled.

'Please tell me what is what.'

Anna began. As she touched each item she called its name, then explained the use. And Chiaku would exclaim: 'True!' or would nod and her eyes would open wide. Then, suddenly, she stopped looking at the things. Rather, she looked steadily at Anna, from the cheeks down to the breasts, down to the stomach. She was studying her for the signs. What was all the property worth when there was nobody—his own flesh—to inherit it? That was what Chiaku was thinking.

'Mother, what's wrong?' Anna asked.

'Everything, my child,' she replied in a sad tone. 'How long ago did the sickness start?'

'Just this morning. It's nothing—mere tiredness. I've been working very hard in our new house since our return.'

Chiaku sighed. 'I thought it was a happy sickness; that you were beginning to be two bodies.'

*

When it was noon she sent the children home and said she would be back in the evening. But when evening came she announced dramatically to her hosts that she would not be going that day; rather, she would go in the morning. She was bent on demanding from them what they had brought home for her, she added.

After supper that night, Joe took out from one of the trunk boxes two rolls of cloth, of the expensive damask type. 'This is what I bought for you at Abagwa,' he said. 'I've not had the chance all these weeks to open the box and take it out.' Anna brought a bowl half-filled with rice, with a full length of stork fish on top. 'This is for you, Mother,' said she meekly. 'I've a head-tie for you too, but can't open the box now; I'll give it to you before you leave in the morning.'

She surveyed the gifts with her eyes, contemptuously. Then she turned away her face from both the donors and the gifts. What was wrong? they wondered. And soon they knew.

'Keep your cloth,' she said waspishly. 'I know what I want. It isn't cloth.'

He was shattered.

'And you, keep your rice and fish.'

Anna was thunderstruck.

'Mother, what's wrong?' he managed to ask.

'You ought to have known what I would demand of you.'

'And what is it?'

There was a tense interval. 'Where are my grand-children?' Another interval. 'I am not a dead body which wants cloth for its burial,' she grumbled; 'I am a living body and therefore want to see my own blood. Spirits of the righteous dead move about looking for where to get re-incarnated, and yet two of you stay like that. Perhaps you don't want me to be called Big Mother before I die.' She turned and stared at them. She shouted aggressively: 'It's you I'm talking to, Nnanna.'

Anna turned away her face, concealing the tears that filled her eyes. But Joe looked on.

'What did I tell you when last you came to Nade— some years ago?'

There was long silence.

His face had contracted. An embarrassed smile now showed on his lips. There was a furrow on his left cheek. Joe had gone into that unfathomable depth, an inner self, which he sometimes hid with an odd smile. What was it she had said on that occasion? 'It's now I know that Okafo your father, is dead. For his son is only a pulpy pillar which will give away under the weight of an edifice. You are not a man.'

Those were the exact words. And then she began to weep. That was six years ago. The year was 1934. He was visiting Nade for the first time since his departure. He came with the priest; he was still a Mission Boy then. And he was still a bachelor.

She had knelt at his feet and entreated him, in the name of all the dead (she called many names), to return to Umudiobia and restore his father's obi. Amanze was alive then; so also Oji, his maternal uncle. Both of them had come with her to see him. Both spoke to him on the same matter. 'Come home, Father, and let us build up your father's family and mine; let us build up Okoli's obi,' Amanze had said. Amanze spoke in a tone which suggested that the passage of time had removed all ill-feeling between them. Oji was a trifle ponderous: 'You may not have thought of it, my son, but this thing you do is like climbing a palm-tree with a single rope. You are the only son of the family. What would happen if the rope should suddenly snap and break? Though may the gods forbid!' Then Amanze spoke again: 'Come home, please, and reclaim your father's compound, the remains of which are now overgrown by bush. And while he has a son yet alive!'

He was deeply touched by their words, although he gave them the opposite impression. Smiling, he told them he would not stay back if that was what they meant; he must return to Ossa with the priest.

'And when will you come home finally?' she asked with a severe countenance. To that he replied:

'I don't know.'

Then she became hysterical. She spat at him and she called him names. She called him a worthless creature, a tramp, a lunatic, the bane of his father's spirit and the death of his mother. She reminded him how she nearly lost her senses years back when he abandoned her and joined the church and school. But he kept on smiling, grimly. Her words, though crude, had eaten deep into his heart.

It was from that time that there came into Joe that urge common among the adult males of the people: to go back home and identify himself permanently with the kith and kin: to go and build up the obi and keep the ama—the approach to it—open and in a good state. Obi, the small, roomless, unpretentious forehouse in the compound! It symbolized the family, the homestead and continuation of the lineage, as well as all that was best in these. And to keep up and strengthen the obi—and what it meant— was the greatest duty a man owed to his father, dead or living. 'He's not dead who has a son that can continue his obi. But it's death, stark and tragic, if one has no son, or if the son is a vagabond, or a pulpy pillar which will crumble under the weight of the edifice.' That was a common, if indelicate, saying, and that was what his mother, Chiaku, told him on that occasion. She had now reminded him of it. . . .

'Take what we've given you,' Joe said dully. 'The children will come one day if it's God's wish.'

'When the ground has met with the sky, is it?' she answered. 'Please show me where to sleep and let me go and lie down.' She rose. 'Isn't it nearly three years now since you were married?'

The next morning she ransacked one of the trunk boxes and removed a pair of earrings, a necklace and a brass bangle.

'These I have decided to take,' she declared, smiling, and held out the articles. 'Give me the ones you showed me last night.'

They both laughed.

'You find it funny, do you?' she said, and then promised them another raid, before the new moon would appear in the sky. As for what she had said in the night, Chiaku had no regrets at all. For it was her belief that such taunts would annoy the son's wife into being a mother.

Five

SHE CAME AGAIN twelve days later. This time she was accompanied by Chinwe alone. She brought a long basket which was half filled with yams. The remaining half contained sliced cassava food, a pot of palm oil, vegetables, and a chicken the legs of which were tied to the basket with soft banana string.

'Where's Nnanna?' asked she as soon as she had sat down.

'He left for Ossa early in the morning,' Anna replied. 'I expect he'll be back in the evening. But, Mother, don't call him Nnanna again,' she added, smiling. 'His name is Joseph.'

Chiaku nodded sarcastically. 'I might as well call him Osofulu.'

'It's easy.'

'I know.' She paused. 'You church men answer all sorts of funny names. Nduru, Ji-Oji, Ji-maimai. In Nade there's even one they call Ofekito. And, to make matters worse, the man is truly three times a fool.'

They all laughed. Chinwe laughed loudest and longest, which Chiaku did not like.

'Look at her!' she remonstrated. 'She laughs like an animal. Don't you remember you are a girl, eh?'

'Leave her alone, she's just happy,' Anna pleaded.

Chiaku pushed the basket forward. 'That's for you, my

daughter. I should have brought you much more, but of late we've been having a series of funeral ceremonies and we do practically nothing other than cooking food for the guests. The chicken there'—she pointed—'is for you to rear. I'll know from it what luck you have with livestock.'

'Thank you, Mother,' Anna replied and drew the basket to her feet, and began to remove the contents. . . then she untied the chicken. She raised it up and inspected it. It was a healthy-looking bird about two months old, its plumage beautifully patterned in golden brown and grey. Anna stroked it gently, fondly, with the palm of her right hand. Then she handed it over to Chinwe.

Chinwe went outside and tethered the chicken to a big stick, and left it under a shed.

*

'Have you brought her now to stay with me?' Anna asked some hours later.

'Ask her, she will answer for herself,' Chiaku replied. 'If she agrees I'd not object. And her father does not object either.'

'You will stay with me, won't you?'

'Yes,' Chinwe confirmed with obvious enthusiasm. Then, as if to leave no doubt in their minds about her decision, she walked across to Anna and clung to her.

'You still go about naked! I better find you something to wear right away.'

She went and brought a piece of cloth from her room. She began to wrap it round Chinwe's waist. Chinwe stood stiff and silent, and docile, as would a customer being measured for a new dress.

'Mother, see!' she beamed.

'He-i!' Chiaku exclaimed gratefully. 'She looks as if

she has been abroad. Show me your back....Yes, you look as if you go to church.' She turned to Anna. Her tone changed. 'I must warn you, don't take her to church.'

Anna said nothing. She just smiled. It was a dull, deceitful smile. She had already decided in her mind. She would take Chinwe to church; she would do that the following Sunday. And she would teach her to knit and to sew. She would teach her how to cook and how to keep the house.

*

The weather suddenly dulled and the sun was no longer visible in the sky. The atmosphere was still.

Thunder began to rumble and lightning flashed too. Then a moderate wind began to blow. Shortly after, a shower came. But it was a light one—a stingy spray much of which was caught on the foliage; what reached the ground made patches of the dust.

'I have to go,' Chiaku said, and rose. 'When he returns tell him I waited the whole day.'

'Why not stay the night and go tomorrow morning instead?' Anna suggested. 'Don't you see the weather is going to be bad?'

'Perhaps I had better watch it for a time in case the drizzle stops.'

They continued to talk.

'I hope you were not very much upset by what I said last time.'

Anna's face turned grave.

'It's only because I'm anxious to have my own grand-children, that's why I spoke like that, daughter. He is an only son in the family. But he must have told you everything already?'

She looked on in silence.

'You must come to Nade and stay with me for some days. I would like to observe you myself. But tell me, do you drink white man's hot wine—the one that stings in the mouth?'

She shook her head.

'Good. Avoid it like poison, please. And avoid anything that is peppery. Avoid juicy fruits. These things either set the womb on fire or disorganise it badly. And remember, do not eat eggs. I know some church men allow their wives to do that, but it's against custom; a woman mustn't eat eggs. Nobody who expects something from the gods should deliberately offend against custom. Does that amuse you?'

Anna stopped laughing.

Chiaku was really angry. She rose and announced that she was leaving. And before Anna could say a word she had already left the house.

Anna followed.

They were now about three hundred yards from the entrance.

'Goodbye, Mother; let me go back to the house.'

'I won't say anything again. I don't want to be laughed at a second time.'

Just then, the drizzle increased. Anna turned and ran.

'What am I seeing!'

She stopped, looked back.

'What was it you were doing?'

She was nearly startled. 'When?'

'Didn't I see you running?'

Her face showed a guilty expression.

'Just what I was saying. Come nearer.'

For a good five minutes, mindless of the drizzle, Chiaku told Anna the story of a certain woman at Obizi who ran faster than many of the men. 'And what was the result?

She had no issue—not until corns had started to eat up the sole of her feet.'

*

'But this one about not eating eggs!' Anna said, the usual smile leaking out from the corner of her mouth.

'You are bound to obey it,' he mumbled.

They were eating supper.

'So that you can eat them alone?'

'There's a way out of it—for you I mean.'

'Tell me.'

'You can forbid the hens to lay again. I would then have no eggs to eat.'

They both laughed. Then some time passed in silence.

'She's kind.'

'You mean Mother?'

'Yes.'

'I told you.'

'If only she would stop talking so harshly to people at times.'

'That's her nature. Nobody can beat her for kindness, provided she has no cause to get angry with you.'

Then Joe told Anna about some incidents of his boyhood days.

'One day I decided to plug my ears with the fingers so as not to hear the torrent that poured from her mouth.'

She laughed.

'Do you know what she did in reply?'

'Tell me.'

'She pulled out my hands and shouted into the ears. "Evil child, that's your latest, is it?" she said and slapped me on the forearm. That was when I had just jointed the church.'

Anna laughed until pepper nearly ran down her throat.

'How was the journey to Ossa?'

'Very good. I'll go again next week.' He paused. 'I think our plans will work, Anna.'

Six

THEY HAD AGREED on plans for their future before they left Abagwa. She would establish a dress-making workshop. It would, almost certainly, be the first of its type in Umudiobia and around. And she would introduce new styles in women's dresses, just as she had at Abagwa. There, at Abagwa, she was popularly known as the Forest Guard's wife who did wonders with the sewing machine, and people came to her shed in large numbers. This was specially so during Christmas and Easter, when mothers made dresses for themselves and for their children. In those two seasons her machine would whir tirelessly until the early hours of morning. And she had many apprentices, too—brides-to-be whom their fiancés sent to her for training. The dress she herself wore was a model to the women of Abagwa. . . . All that she owed to Agatha, and to the convent at Ossa, Anna often reflected.

It was with a sense of sacrifice that Anna agreed to leave Abagwa and all it meant to her, and it had not been easy to get her to make the sacrifice. When first Joe told her about his intention to return to Umudiobia, she merely laughed: she thought he was joking. But then he kept on talking about it—nearly every day and in a serious tone, until one day she was compelled to ask:

'Do you mean what you're saying, Joe?'

'Of course,' he replied.

Some interval passed in silence. 'What about your job?'

'I will resign.'

'You will do what?'

Then he began to explain. He planned to grow a rubber plantation at Umudiobia. Rubber was in very great demand, just like palm-oil and kernel, because of the war. The District Officer had had it announced, time without number, that the two things—rubber and palm produce—were indispensable if the war against Hitler was to be won. . . . Yes, he was sure they would be well off in Umudiobia if they had a large rubber plantation there. He knew of people who had become rich because of rubber. 'And being a Forest Guard, I should be in a better position than any to grow the trees.'

Anna clicked her tongue. 'That could be true. But is that why you should resign your post?'

He observed her face furtively. It was gloomy. Anna looked like one in distress. He could understand. She was very proud of the position he held, very proud of the way he held it. That she had, in an unguarded moment one day, not long before, told him. She liked, Anna had said, the forest-green shirt and shorts, the black boots and black straps, the broad leather belt round his waist—but not the beret cap. What she liked most was the precious metal stamp. No timber or wood could be sold which had not the impress of that stamp. More than that, the owner of such timber would be arrested and charged to court. At the end of each day, he would hand the stamp over to her for safe keeping; and she would keep it under her pillow. Then, in the morning, she would return it to him; and she would observe him as he put it inside his pocket. That gave her the feeling that she shared in his work. And, to add to it all, he had made a good name for himself, and for her, by his integrity and sincerity. No wonder he was able to rise to the rank of

Chief Forest Guard in just five years, and other women were jealous of her. All that Anna had told him on that day.

'Let's not talk about it again—not today at least,' Joe retreated. 'Forget about it!'

But she still looked unhappy. She began to hum, singing to herself.

He rose and went to the kitchen.

He returned a few minutes later.

'This fish is quite tasty.' He spoke like a masquerade.

Anna turned. She forced herself to smile. And with that, her countenance began to thaw. . . .

Four whole weeks passed before he spoke to her again about it. And this time he told her the remaining half of the truth. There was rumour that all able-bodied Government employees at Ania, Ossa and Abagwa were going to be conscripted into the army. That year, 1939, over forty persons were known to have been conscripted at Ania alone. The thing would soon be extended to other parts of the District. He was able-bodied, that was sure; there was therefore no likelihood of his being left out. The conscripts were sent to the Middle East, or to India, or to Burma, and nobody was sure they would survive the war in which countless numbers were killed each day.

'I'm an only son, remember. I can't take the risk. I must resign at once.'

For some minutes she would not speak. She just stared at him. Then: 'Why can't we stay here when you resign?'

He shrugged. 'What would I be doing?'

Anna pondered: 'Or we can go to Ania, or even Ossa. This Umudiobia you're talking about—'

'I'm sure the D.O. will be happy to hear that I'm going home to start my own rubber plantation, and therefore will accept my resignation readily. Don't you see what I mean?'

Silence.

44

'In any case, I have a hometown. We had better return there. Let me go and restore my father's homestead at least.'

She made no reply, just watched him out of the corners of her eyes.

His face was grave and thoughtful.

'And not only rubber, I shall also try to trade.'

'In what?'

'Anything. Salt, for example. And you, you can establish a dress-making workshop as you've done here.' He paused. 'Or would you rather have me conscripted?'

A pause. Then Anna stood up, shaking her head resolutely. She swore, bitterly. 'May God set the D.O. on fire! You will not go into any army. How can they take you away and leave me alone? You'd better resign at once if it is that. I'm sure we can manage.'

Three days later, he gave notice of his resignation.

*

He left at second cock-crow, on his bicycle, for Ossa. It was only twenty-five miles away, yet she did not expect him back before sunset as the road was so bad.

It started even and broad, and smooth. It continued like that for six miles, when you came to Obizi. There, a fork to the left led to Abagwa, fifty miles off. The right fork led to Ania along the big flowing water. From Obizi onwards the road was rugged and winding, with a series of steep rises and gentle falls, until you came to Ossa on a hill. It took several hours by bicycle to cover the distance but the return journey was a matter of two or three hours, a pleasurable descent in which the bicycle hummed jubilantly and the woods vibrated with the noise.

Daylight was fast merging with darkness but there was no sign of him. Anna stood in the entrance and stared into the distance, beginning to feel that something must have gone wrong. Then:

'Tim-go tim-go tim-go!'

She ran out. A few moments later she grabbed the bicycle from him and wheeled it towards the house.

'I hope you went well.'

'Very well indeed. Did anything go amiss in my absence?'

'Yes, everything!' She giggled. 'You think that once you leave the house everything—including the sand we walk on—begins to misbehave!'

As soon as he was seated, she brought him a meal, a big plate of rice, urging him to eat. 'Finish the whole plate.'

'I'll do my best.'

She watched him fondly.

'Did you buy what I asked you to?'

'Yes, I did, even though you didn't give me the money for that.'

'Let's see it.'

'Look inside the bag on the bicycle carriage.'

She found inside the bag a packet of biscuits and a tin of corned beef, in addition to the sewing thread she had ordered.

'Is all this for me, Joe?' she exclaimed gratefully.

'Not at all. Part of it is for your husband's second wife.'

'Oh, when is she arriving?'

'When the sky meets the ground.'

They both laughed.

He told her more about the journey. He told her he had arranged for supply of rubber seeds.

'When do you start the plantation?'

'Soon.'

'What does that mean?'

'Probably next year. We have to clear the site first.'

'And what about the trade in salt?'

'I've arranged for that too. I was registered today as a dealer. That means I can go to Ossa once a week to buy up to five bags of salt from the District Office.'

'And what about my own?'

'What?'

'I mean the dress-making. When do we build the work-shop?'

'That will also be done soon.'

'We're wasting time, Joe,' she said. 'It's nearly a year since we returned, and yet we've not started. But for the small sewing I've been doing in the house, my machine would have got rusty by now.'

'Look, I've nearly finished,' said Joe, trying to change the subject.

'Well done. But what about what I was saying?'

He laughed. 'You are the proverbial tortoise.'

'Which did what?'

'It lost its patience on the very day it was to be released, after it had been imprisoned for several years in a refuse dump.'

'That's not a proverb; you've just made it up.' She had never trusted his knowledge of proverbs.

*

He made it a habit to visit Ossa once a week. He would leave early in the morning and return when the sun had begun to set. One day he came home to find both Anna and Chinwe out. After a time he began to wonder where they were. Then Obieke, carrying a jar of palm-wine, came in, followed by Uzondu. The jar explained why Uzondu was following so closely.

'You are welcome, Father,' said Obieke and put the jar down and took his seat. 'I felt you would be thirsty on your return, so I brought this.'

'Many thanks, brother,' Joe replied. 'As you say, I'm very thirsty. Please pour it out.'

'What is it the proverb says?' Uzondu said.

'You tell us,' Obieke said.

'The Udala fruit drops of its own accord when it sees a worthy person passing. Your wine has dropped on us, Obieke.' His face expanded into a smile. The other two laughed.

Obieke began to pour out the wine. 'Uzondu my brother, did you say you were a worthy man?'

'Why not? And the two of you, too.'

'We are not, you alone are. But tell us, what have you done to merit the description?'

'That's true. I've done nothing—nothing bad. But where's our wife?'

'You've just remembered her, have you?'

Joe said: 'I haven't seen her. Did you?'

'Oh yes, she's in my house. She's plaiting Akueze's hair.'

'She's going to make your wife look like one who has been abroad!' Uzondu cried.

'Why not? What did you think of me?' Obieke replied. 'He whose brother has been abroad must look better than others—and his wife should also.'

'That I can see already. You no longer tie a strip of cloth—at least not always; you now dress as if you go to church. I shouldn't be surprised if you begin to wear trawusa, the one that covers the whole of the legs.'

Obieke smiled. Joe laughed. Uzondu continued to stare at the jar.

'Pour the wine, please.'

Obieke poured into the cup and handed over to him, then reverted to the subject of Anna and Akueze.

'My only fear is that the good woman is wasting her time on Akueze. She's my own wife, Akueze is, but when I see something that is evil I say it out. She does not deserve anything good.'

'Patience, that's what women need,' Joe said philosophically.

'Not just that, my brother. My wife requires deafness too.' He smiled grimly.

'I agree with you, Obieke,' Uzondu said. He had just emptied the third cup. 'She's pepper. Three days ago she nearly beat your son, Obiakizu, to death. I saw her with my eyes. Pour the wine, please.'

Obieke poured absent-mindedly, with the result that the wine brimmed over.

'She's been doing worse things,' said he. 'And yet I married her so that she would look after the boy. I did not know that I was bringing misfortune into my house.' He paused, then resumed in a solemn, distressed tone: 'Mgbafo, Obiakizu's mother, was a good woman—everybody knew that. She died at child-birth, leaving me with the small child.' He paused again. 'Yes, I married Akueze in the hope that she would look after the child. She does the opposite. It was for her sake that I sent Obiakizu away to his grandmother's house last year. He returned only a few days ago, and since then she would not let him move about freely in his own father's house.' He paused the third time. He turned round. 'See the scar there. See. It's a wound that woman gave me some time ago. But she will meet her deserts one day. Please tell Anna to mind how she goes with her.'

'And you people still want Uzondu to marry, don't you?' Uzondu asked.

'Oko-o-o-ko-o!' he called several times.

In a few minutes Obiakizu ran in, panting. There was a friendly smile on his face and his eyes shone with life. Joe regarded him steadily. He was a plump, handsome boy, nearly five years old. He had a big, protruding navel which looked rather like a tennis ball.

'Big pot!' Uzondu touched the navel.

'Fat one!' Obiakizu beat off the hand.

'Did you know he's your father?'

'So I hear,' replied Joe. 'Although he looks too small to be a father.'

'You church men don't believe that the dead are re-incarnated, I know.'

'No, we don't.'

'You better do.'

Obieke interrupted: 'Run to the house, Obiakizu, and call your son's wife.'

'Who?' asked he with a surprised tone.

'Don't you know who is your son's wife?'

'O-o-oh! I have understood.'

'Run faster than a dog, and tell her that your son is back. She's wanted immediately.'

*

By the time she arrived another person had joined the party. It was Willie, and he had already begun to say very un-complimentary things about white men in general, and the missionaries in particular. She sighed painfully.

Willie spoke with unusual vehemence today, with the result that sweat soaked both arm-pits.

' . . . They came out to Africa to eat chickens and eggs. Those things cannot be found in their country,' he declared.

'Why do you people listen to him?' Anna now objected, frowning.

'No, you had better leave him to run out,' Joe said.

'Of course I'm not surprised,' he went on, smiling obstinately. '"Religion is the opium of the people." That's what a certain wise man once said. I would amend that: it's the opium of women. Anyway, when we begin to rule ourselves—'

'Willie, please allow us to drink our wine in peace,' Uzondu said.

'—we won't let them go on like that.'

'Will you shut up, my friend!' demanded Obieke, his elder brother.

'We want our own church and nothing—'

'Why don't you go back to Ania and talk to your followers there,' Joe said, amused and angry at the same time. 'I'm sure you can't convince anybody here in Umudiobia. And stop saying such things in my house, anyway.'

'I hear your people are expecting Father George back at Obizi,' he persisted. 'He's the first man we'll remove from this area as soon as we become free. May I have some of the wine?'

'May it choke you to death!' Anna swore, inwardly. Whatever was his crime, it would have been a grievous offence on her part to say it aloud. And it would have cost her a white-feathered hen, quite difficult to procure, in addition to other things.

Seven

OBIZI PARISH was established three years back. It comprised Obizi itself, Ujiji, Ozala, Uzi, Nade, Umudiobia, and towns to the south as far as to Ogolo, the land of bread-fruit trees. Twenty-seven in all. It was Father Dennis George himself who started it, after which he returned to Ania along the river. Since then nobody had seen him again in the area. And now, he was being expected back. He would take charge of the parish.

In the short time he was there, Father George had made a name for himself among the natives—converts and non-converts, Catholics and non-Catholics. He won the nickname of 'The-very-short-one-more-powerful-than-any-twice-his-height'. For he was decidedly of a low stature, though of strong physique and boundless energy. 'It is an injection he had during the first white man's war—the one that preceded the influenza—which made him so strong,' some would say. Some others maintained that he actually killed a famous German soldier (unnamed) in that war; and that if the Pope had allowed him to fight in the present one Hitler would have been vanquished long ago.

Of the several incidents that took place during his stay in the parish, two were especially remarkable.

The first was at Ogolo. That town was celebrating the feast of Mgbede which usually was the greatest event in the year. In the general excitement, the orgy of feasting and dancing, the converts put aside all they had been taught about pagan festivals and the First Commandment, and joined in the celebrations. The men raced with masquerades; the women painted their skins brown; the girls danced before Mgbede's shrine. That was in addition to the festival meals which they had eaten. There were however a few among them who would have nothing to do with the celebrations. These went to Obizi and reported to the priest.

Father George arrived in Ogolo on his motor-cycle panting, silent. He beat the church tom-tom hard and hastily. He beat it again, again, again. . . . Thirty minutes passed and yet only a handful had assembled in answer to the tom-tom beats. Another thirty minutes passed. Father George declared the church in Ogolo dead. Then he struck a match and set the thatch roof on fire. And the house burnt to the ground. Ogolo had since repented and been allowed to rebuild the church. But the neighbours made an unkind joke out of the event. From that time, said they, the people of Ogolo cut down on breadfruit meals—the devil which had lured them into the celebrations.

The second incident took place only a few days after, this time at Obizi. One Rev. J. J. Godson, of the New Apostolic World Christian Congregation, had referred to Father George as the militant Irish fellow that looked as if he was going to burst into pieces at any moment and who wanted the whole of the continent of Africa for his church alone. A new man in the place, Godson was as yet ignorant of the methods of rival sects; he did not know that there were among his audience, or supposed converts, spies from the other churches in the area.

Father George was terribly hurt when the story got to him later that day, more so perhaps because the description was very close to the truth.

One day Rev. Godson's motor-cycle ran out of petrol. He sent his catechist to Father George to ask for assistance.

'You want my petrol, do you?' Father George asked in a calm voice when the catechist had finished relating his mission.

'Yes, Sir.'

'Ha-ha-ha! Friend, run away from here,' he laughed, pointing towards the road with the spanner in his hand. 'At once!'

'But—'

He roared: 'Off at once, fellow. Tell that protestant, Devilson or whatever he calls himself, to protest against my petrol too.'

How the story came to spread nobody could say, but the next day nearly every town in the parish was talking about it. And some added salt. 'The Rev. Father had actually ordered Godson to leave the land,' they said. And, as if to confirm that, Godson was soon assaulted by malaria and was compelled to leave. He never returned. And his church wound up in a matter of weeks.

*

The church bell sounded: 'Gbam gbam gbam-gbam-gbam. . . .'

'Ready?'

'Almost,' replied Anna from her room. Then she undid her head-tie, for the fifth time.

'Don't let us be late.' He went out to the front yard.

One thing he hated was to be delayed and she knew this only too well. She came through into the sitting-room, and she looked out at him. Good, he didn't look upset. Not yet at least.

'You will please allow me to finish. I only have to tie my head-tie. And besides, isn't it only just seven o'clock?'

'Hurry up.'

'You wouldn't like me to look like a mad woman, would you?'

'If you choose to, I will not object.' He smiled and she giggled. 'Remember Father George is coming to say Mass here for the first time since his arrival. We may not have seats if we don't get there in good time.'

She came out to the front yard. 'I'm ready now. Oh, no! I didn't powder my face. Please, just one second.' She ran in.

He began to sing the Kyrie eleison.

'Hoarse voice!' Anna called from within, not unfairly. He persisted. Then he stopped, suddenly.

'What's wrong?'

'What?'

'Not you; I'm speaking to Obiakizu. What's wrong?'

'It's Akueze,' Obiakizu whined. He was now walking across, towards the house. He rubbed his wrist over the eyes.

'What did she do to you?'

He faltered: 'She hit me with a stick.'

'Where?'

'At the back.'

Joe held him by the shoulders and looked. His countenance saddened. The weal ran across the hollow of the child's back. 'Anna, please come and see this.'

When she saw the wound she let out a sigh and her face contracted. Then she ran her palm soothingly over the child's back, avoiding the weal. 'What made her hit you like this?'

'Nothing,' Obiakizu answered. 'She said I didn't sweep the yard.'

'Is that why she should beat you as if you were a robber?'

'Let him stay here until we return—there's no need for him to go back there now,' she proposed.

'We could even take him to church, though I doubt whether Obieke will like it.'

'Who knows?' She went in and brought a yard of cloth which was, substantively, a head-tie. She tied it on Obiakizu's neck and let it drape down his body.

They had not gone far from the house when they saw Obieke. They began to explain and Obieke listened calmly. Then, when they had finished, he frowned in protest and demanded his son back, in a surprisingly brusque manner. He would not let anybody take his first son to the church, Obieke declared. They delivered Obiakizu into his hand. Then they quickened their steps.

Joe wore a light-grey tussore suit, brown leather shoes and a dark-grey hat. A shining metal chain looped from the lapel into the breast-pocket of his coat. She wore a flowered silk dress and a pair of low heeled black shoes. They walked side by side and they conversed, which was rather a curiosity in a land where the women kept a long distance, usually in front of, their husbands.

Soon a group of children, very much impressed, began to follow quite close behind. They commented on the attire which, said they, must have cost nearly a pound. They also talked about the day when the lorry, Psalm 25, brought the two home. Some noted, there and then, that the couple would make very good hosts for Christmas. A good number clapped the soles of their feet on the ground in wishful imitation of shod steps.

These children belonged to two different religious sects— Catholic and Anglican. They were to part at the road fork near the market square, the Catholics to the east and the Anglicans further north. But long before they got there, they became conscious, in a practical way, of the fact that they belonged to rival groups.

It started with a sort of impromptu and open-air religious debate.

'You people are happy because your short Father has come back, and is visiting you today.'

'Why not?' retorted a Catholic boy. 'You better warn your pastor. If he doesn't behave himself Father will order him out as he did the Apostolic man.'

'I hear you will receive Communion today and have been starving for a week now.' Someone amended: 'They eat quite all right, but they rinse their mouth thoroughly so that Father can't find out.'

'You eat bananas in your own church, don't you?'

Joe smiled indulgently and glanced at Anna. She was frowning; she was taking the thing too seriously. He urged her to quicken her steps, which she did.

The boys followed still dangerously close.

'Your headmaster is as tiny as string.'

'That's true,' conceded a Catholic boy. 'And your own headmaster's wife beats him everyday.'

'Are you people serious when you say a woman gave birth to God?'

Anna winced and almost halted. Joe reminded her that they were in a hurry.

'Fool! Look at your pastor! He orders you to close your eyes for prayers and when you've done so he steals the church collection.'

'Yes, your Father tells you he's not married whereas he keeps his wife and children in his country.'

That was the limit! Anna turned round and shouted 'Shut up!' But the order had little or no effect on the children, partly because only a small number heard her tiny voice, and partly because, being boys, they were not used to being hush-ed by women like that. They went on arguing and shouting, with increasing vehemence. And their voices rang far and with barbaric shrillness.

'. . . The man who began your church had eight wives. Deny that.'

'You are not allowed to read the Bible. Your Father is afraid you will discover God's true word and dispense with his services. Deny that.'

'Vagabond!'

'Judas Carrot! . . .'

'Why did you push me?'

'He punched my nose!'

Joe turned at last. He found the boys already drawn up for a real religious war. He went closer. He saw two boys—probably Vagabond and Judas Carrot—already tearing each other to pieces. 'Stop, stop!' Joe ordered and set about to separate the fighters. And he succeeded.

'I thought you boys were joking; I didn't know you took the things you were saying to heart,' said he in rebuke.

Then from a distance someone commended: 'You are a good man, friend. Please prevent them from killing each other.' He was a wiry-looking, elderly man. His eyelids were painted white and there were rings of thread on his wrists and ankles. He ground his teeth sorrowfully, then continued, in an agitated tone: 'That's what we find in Umudiobia these days. Brothers fight one another and would not even attend one another's funeral or marriage. Just because they go to different churches!' Then he began to rummage in the bag which hung down from his left shoulder.

They all watched. He took out something—a small black idol. The children drew back. He touched the idol lightly on the ground and he prayed aloud, to the spirits of the dead ancestors. He prayed that the spirits should wipe out all churches from the land and reconcile brother to brother. Then the children booed, and mocked, without any regard for his age. And they called him names. They asked how many chickens he had collected that morning. For they knew he was a priest-doctor.

*

The Father's kit-car was already in the church premises before Joe and Anna arrived. The priest had retired into his rest house—a small one-room stone building at the farthest end of the compound, remote from the noises. Also a large crowd of children had gathered round the car. As usual, they were now jeering at the images, distorted on reflection, which they saw in the shiny metal parts. Some pointed, some grimaced, some grinned—just to see what the monsters would do in retaliation. 'See, my head is big and flat,' they said, staring into the chromium-plated wheel-cover. One boy was actually addressing a stern rebuke to his own image: 'You tadpole! So you think you are myself? . . . '

The bigger ones made to climb in at the back. Last time the car came the driver had taken them into the town on a ride. Later on, they had gone round to challenge their cousins in other churches to produce their own car and ride in it. They had hoped the same thing would happen today, and that was why they wanted to climb in. But the driver wasn't going to allow them—he would not even let them touch the vehicle with their fingers. Naturally, they wondered why he was so narrow-minded today.

The bell rang again. 'Gbam gbam gbam . . . '—a steady, hasty monotone. They stampeded towards the church, some dragging their younger brothers or sisters, and crushed through into the building.

There was great confusion when Joe and Anna entered. The children were trying to find their seats and were shouting or crying in the process. The church-wardens, all physically fit and armed with canes, were either hushing them, or beating order into them, or twisting their ears. Anna went to the left side where the women sat. She succeeded in finding a comfortable seat. But not so readily did Joe. The men's side was packed full, except at the pew in the fore-front which Jerome, the Pillar, and any he cared to welcome to it, usually occupied. There was still space there for one but nobody had so far had the courage to occupy it. Joe went to this space.

Jerome turned stiffly and regarded him severely for a few seconds.

Father George walked into the church a few moments later. He came in from the side door which led to the altar space. For some seconds he stood silent and immovable, facing the congregation. Anger had transformed him into a statue. If there was anything he hated in the people more than paganism, it was noise-making, especially when that was inside a church. Knowing this full well, the church wardens worked harder than ever before. They swished their canes, they shouted threats and swear words, and they harassed mothers with children in their arms. But none of this did much to help.

'Stop shouting!' the priest bellowed, his voice booming over the noises.

The voices began to subside.

'Wawu wawu wawu!' he barked in mimicry, exposing his toothless lower jaw.

Umudiobia, christian or pagan, had a high and un-inhibited sense of humour. Somebody remarked that the jaw resembled the posterior of a plucked chicken. Another wondered how the priest managed with bones. Then, from the women's side of the church, a child cried: 'Mamma, does he eat only fou fou?'

All this happened at once. The congregation burst into uncontrollable laughter, even though thirty volunteers, including five women, rose spontaneously to assist the wardens while Jerome threatened that he would get all the wardens changed in a week. What really saved the situation was the headmaster's common sense. For he called a song, a catchy tune in which nearly everyone joined. Even then, Father George was able to pick out seven people who were still talking. Among them was a mother who was feeding her baby with breast-milk. He ordered the seven to kneel down in front of the altar, with their back at the congregation. They were to remain kneeling till the end of the Mass, he said.

*

He spoke powerfully during the sermon. First, quite predictably, he reminded them about the sins against the First Commandment—divination, sacrifices, juju, charms, belief in dreams and other forms of superstition. The catechist interpreted.

Then he spoke about polygamy. 'I know this has been a source of temptation to many converts in this part of the world. . . . Especially when their wives do not give them male children, or any at all. . . . It is on that rock that many a man's faith has foundered beyond rescue. But those are people who haven't sufficient faith.'

'Let me warn,' he cried and pointed both fore-fingers at the congregation, his eyes flashing. It seemed indeed as if he was about to burst. For although he was short, he was stout and solidly built. 'I shall not tolerate a thing like that in this parish. It were better for such a one never to have been born at all than even to contemplate a thing like that.'

The catechist paused, licked his lips for no apparent reason. 'It would have been better for the man who betrayed Our Lord not to have been born at all,' he said in the vernacular.

'Translate what I said and don't you preach your own sermon. You hear me?'

'Yes, Father. Sorry, Father.'

Eight

HE HAD RETURNED from Ossa at nightfall, and he was unusually tired now. He sat on a straw mat spread on the floor, and leaned with his back against the wall, his legs stretched. Anna sat at the opposite end of the sitting-room. She was sewing while they talked. A hurricane lamp was burning on the table, close to the sewing-machine. It was well after supper and the night was very dark. Somewhere in the bush an owl was hooting. The sound added a fearful, ghostly quality to the darkness.

Suddenly she stamped her foot on the floor, child-like. She slapped her hand lightly on the machine. 'O-o-oh! What's wrong with me whom they call Anna!' she cried.

'Mind my floor; you can treat your machine as you please,' Joe said.

She hissed in self-reproach.

'What's the matter anyway?'

'I went on running the needle on the cloth. I didn't know it has no more thread.'

He laughed. 'I'm sure you're fagged out now. You had better stop for the night.'

'I think you're right, I've been sewing all day. I just wanted to complete this dress before going to bed.'

Anna left the table and went and sat on a chair, quite close to him.

'Listen to Chinwe snoring.'

'Awful. Go in and move her head.'

'No need asking whom she resembles,' she teased, and after that she went in, smiling.

When she returned she said: 'Joe, that girl resembles you in nearly every respect—the way she talks, the way she walks, and even the way she lies in bed.'

'She's lucky then.'

'Indeed! There's only one thing in which she's very much unlike you.'

'What could that be?'

'I won't tell you.'

'Am I anxious to know?'

She paused. 'You've been getting too moody of late,' said she to him, seriously. 'What's the cause?'

'That's not true.'

'Yesterday, for example. Anyway, how was the journey to Ossa?'

'Very good,' said he. 'I bought eight bags of salt and do you know what happened to them?'

'Yes?'

'I've sold all of them out.'

'True?'

He told her the details. He was fortunate to meet at Ossa a lorry which was travelling to Obizi. He put the bags, together with his bicycle, in the lorry. When he reached Obizi he saw very many people, old and young, rushing towards a small shop where salt was sold. A cup of salt cost as much as two pence there, and yet there was so much scramble! On enquiry, he discovered what had happened. Somebody, probably the owner of the shop, had started a rumour that the Germans had just sunk ten big ships which were loaded with salt, and which were bound for Ania; and that there would be no further supply for another four months. He himself also took advantage of the rumour and sold the eight bags, making a profit of two pounds fifteen shillings.

Anna said a few words in praise of those that started the war.

'Joe, do you think Father George had us in mind when he was preaching that sermon?' she asked.

'Why? No!' he snapped.

'I believe he did.'

He shook his head. 'I hear that's his habit,' said he in a weary, distant tone. 'Everywhere he goes he must preach about idols and polygamy.'

'Who told you?'

'Someone I met at Ossa today. We used to be good friends and now he is a teacher there. I told him we now have Father George in the parish and he exclaimed: "Father Polygamy!"'

She smiled, grimly, reluctantly. 'That may be, but didn't you notice people looking at us as he spoke?'

'Who were?'

'Many people.'

He opened his mouth, closed it. He shook his head. 'I didn't see them.'

'They did.'

'It's your imagination. But what would it have mattered if they did?'

She hesitated. 'Please listen to what I'm going to say now.'

'What again?'

'I know you don't usually want to discuss anything about it but I'll try to convince you: let's begin to look for a good native doctor over here.'

He was silent.

'Please.'

He rose from the mat and walked towards his room.

'Have I upset you?'

'Not that, it's time we went in to sleep.'

She returned to her machine.

It was past midnight before she slept that night.

*

The amount of work she had was now more than could be done part-time and at home. For she was well-known even outside Umudiobia, as the one who sewed better than any and had not time to mend old dresses. And besides, there were many who were anxious to send apprentices to her for training. As yet she had been able to take in only four, of whom Chinwe was one. Considering all these, Anna suggested and Joe agreed that it was time she had her workshop at a conspicuous place, near the market-square.

There was a small piece of land only a few yards from the market square, situated along the big road which ran into the town from Obizi. This land, so small that it could take only two hundred mounds of yams, or even less, had belonged to Okoli. How that happened nobody could tell, for it was far removed from the rest of the family land. Some believed it was given to him by his father, Udemezue, as a special favour; for Okoli was a dear child and the soil was extremely fertile. Obieke had cultivated the land the year before and had dug out from it tubers that people rushed to see.

It was on this site that Joe wanted Anna's workshop built.

Obieke was agreeable. In fact, it was he who arranged for labour to clear the bush and stump and level the ground. Obieke also offered to provide a good part of the raffia mat that would be required for the roof. But his wife, Akueze, felt differently.

'What is it I hear you intend to do with that land near the market square?' Akueze demanded.

'Why do you ask?'

'Because I want to know.' She scowled at him.

'What you ought first to know is that it's our grandfather's land and therefore belongs to him more than to me.'

She turned her back to him. 'Tfia!' she spat. 'Just because they give you hot wine to drink!'

That happened in Obieke's obi. Anna chanced to be passing near the entrance door at the time and she overheard. And later that day she told Joe about it, who advised her to pretend she had not heard. Anna was quite able to pretend. But from that day she avoided Akueze's company.

It took nearly three months before the shed was ready for use. For the red-earth floor had to be beaten down for weeks, then allowed to dry. Then two bamboo stalls were erected within, and the necessary furniture provided. There were two long tables and four benches, a small table and four stools all of which were made by an expert carpenter at Obizi.

Within two weeks of the opening, as many as twenty apprentices were enrolled at the workshop. They were mostly brides-to-be, just as at Abagwa. The fee was six pence a month, yet they were all glad to pay, at least in those early months.

They all wore a yellow uniform—gowns for younger, unmarried ones and wrapper and blouse for the married. The day would open at eight in the morning, with prayers. From then on, the scissors would champ and the machine whir till it was noon. Then they would go on a break for lunch, and resume at about two o'clock. They would close finally for the day when the sun had set completely.

They often told funny stories while at work, called each

other names and sang. A lone voice would trill and start a hymn to Mary, Mother of God, and the rest would join in. Then the place would be transformed into a female choir; and the humorous men of Umudiobia would wonder whether the group had set up one more church in the town.

The magic that was the sewing-machine often confused the new-comers or filled them with some vague awe. It was with much patience that Anna started such ones off.

'Watch me carefully,' Anna would say. 'And you, you, you . . .'— she pointed—'come and watch too, for I don't think you're doing well yet.'

They would range round the table, the new-comer taking a privileged position on the right side of the teacher.

'You first turn the hand-wheel backward. See. . . . The needle rises and you slide in the cloth. See. . . . Then you turn the wheel again, forward this time. See. . . . The needle comes down on the cloth. See. . . . You turn the handle gently and move the cloth gently, Please note, gently. If not, the needle will break. Watch.'

'Kr-r-r-r. . . .'

They almost invariably did well. But the older members often teased the new-comers and tried to make them nervous. 'Needle-breaker!' they would whisper aloud, sniggering. By that, they were referring to the incident of one particular morning.

'Cecilia, you've been learning how to use the machine for a week now,' Anna had said. 'Let's see you sew this morning.'

Cecilia was a big, muscular girl and they had already nicknamed her Not-fit-to-be-a-girl. When she turned the handle she forgot to shift the cloth. The result was that the needle got jammed and the handle would not move again. She turned harder still, putting her masculine strength into it. (Some said she actually groaned.) Anna came over hurriedly. But it was too late. The needle was already broken. And it was the only one left. They had to close the shed for days. From that day any new-comer was regarded as a potential needle-breaker.

For the children of the land, Anna's workshop had some additional interest. They would hover round while it was in session. As soon as work was over and everybody gone, they would rush in to pick the scraps of cloth left off after work. For they liked the floral designs and geometrical patterns. They took the scraps home as property. And during games they would hold the scraps tightly over their mouths, playing masquerades; and they would pursue one another, in turns, with short sticks in hand. Some would just pin the scraps to the tip of bamboo straw and run about, letting the cloth flutter in the wind. 'Ti-i-i!' they would growl, imitating a lorry engine. 'Run away, my new lorry is coming . . . . Ti-i-i! It was made at the same place with Father's car . . . . Ti-i-i! It will crush you to death if you stand in its way. . . . '

But the older ones looked at the shed from another angle. This woman was very rich, they reasoned. And how could any woman be rich if the husband was not? This was a prosperous couple, well worth a visit during Christmas. Yes, they would pay them a visit during Christmas. Let it rain and they would cover their heads with banana leaves. And if the sun should beat down fiercely they would take narrow, shady footpaths.

Indeed many of them came during Christmas, and they were well feasted. Each went home and told his cousin that Joe and Anna were the kindest hosts in the land; that they served rice as well as yams, meat as well as biscuits. Then the cousin, in turn, came to find things out for himself.

And then a delegation came.

They were six in number and they came from St Barnabas

Catholic School, Umudiobia. Wisely they did not disclose their intention right away—not until they had been feasted. Then one of them spoke. From the fact that he had a bigger share of the thing in the soup than any, Joe was able to deduce that he was their leader.

'We are asking for a donation to buy a new band-set for the school.'

'That's a good idea. About how much do you think the set will cost?' Joe asked.

'The headmaster says ten pounds.'

'And then, we have to buy the uniform too,' another said. And another: 'The headmaster says that it will take another four pounds.'

Joe and Anna conferred briefly.

'All right,' he said. 'We—myself and my wife—have agreed to pay the four pounds for your uniform.'

They clapped.

'We'll give the money to the headmaster in a week or so.'

They applauded. Some hopped up also.

'Or, if he prefers, I can buy the cloth myself when next I visit Ania.'

They yelled and screamed. Some danced. And in the end they embraced each other.

Nine

IT WAS AT the end of their second year in Umudiobia that Joe decided he should build his permanent residence, without further delay. For the small, thatch house was now much below the position in which he was held in the town. But before doing anything he should first inform Obieke and some at least of the kinsmen. Nobody ever built a house alone.

Obieke received the news with great joy—so much that he clapped his hands and jumped up. 'You had better invite our kinsmen and tell them,' Obieke said. 'Everyone of them without exception. And when they come you will let them understand that you'll require their help. . . . '

They all assembled a few days later in response to the invitation. The sun had set and the moon had succeeded, imperceptibly. The moon shone bright and the weather was warm. They sat in the open front-yard. They were a little under thirty. All of them were of marriageable age and above, and most of them had wives and homes of their own.

After kola Joe brought two big jars of palm-wine. They disposed of that in no time. Then Anna brought a big basin filled with rice, with sizeable pieces of meat spread on top. Promptly two people came forward and began to pick the pieces, with both care and respect, into an empty plate. The rest watched and wondered aloud, seriously, what had put the idea into her head. Why did Anna cut the meat up into nearly equal shares, without any regard for seniority?

'It's the way it's done in civilized places,' Willie said. It was his first speech so far.

'What does he mean?' asked several voices together.

'In white man's country,' he tried to explain.

'So the white man is now your friend?'

'All right, Joe, tell her to serve them the whole animal uncut next time,' he snapped.

After the meat and rice, Joe brought a full bottle of gin. He handed it over to Obieke, then sat down. From that point he merely watched the proceeding, one leg crossed over the other, conspicuous in his white shirt.

'Silence, silence, silence!' called Obieke gleefully.

The voices died down. They stared at the bottle, Uzondu the hardest. From an opening in the door Anna peeped out and watched.

'Ta nma nma nu!' Obieke cried, stamping his right foot on the ground. His small frame quivered.

'Yoh!' they answered.

'Nma nma nu!'

'Yoh!'

He growled. There was a silence. 'I say, may the best of everything be found in our land.'

'Ofo!'

Then the ceremony began. The bottle was a precious gift to the family. It must therefore pass through the six main branches of the tree. Udemezue had had seven sons in fact. But one had died without a son and his obi had disappeared and the approach to it was now overgrown by bush. First, the bottle went to Nwokeji, who, though barely thirty years old, was the head of the extended family. What one's chi has given to one nobody should grudge. So nobody grudged Nwokeji whenever he took the first place or the first share. Next, it passed to Obieke, that is, to Okoli's lineage—Okoli being Udemezue's second son. It would have gone to Joe in fact, but Joe was the donor. Then Obieke passed it on to Uzondu. The practice had nothing to do with one's personal qualities—it did not matter at all whether one was rootless or not; the important fact was that Uzondu was the first son of his father. Uzondu held the bottle before him and gazed at it for a long time, so much that Amaechina, his younger brother, dashed forward in anger and snatched it away. Then to Ofomata, and to Ikelionwu. Finally it got to Ikeli. Ironically, Ikeli was the oldest in the gathering. But the fact was there: his father Aka had been Udemezue's youngest son.

They soon began to drink. Each emptied the small quantity poured out for him. Most of them first rinsed their mouth before swallowing down, in the hope that the sharp sting would destroy every trace of tooth-ache.

'If you care to listen—' a voice said. All eyes turned to the direction. Then they hissed in disappointment. It was Ojiako, a man known throughout Umudiobia for his cock and bull stories. They told him to keep the story to himself. But Ojiako went ahead all the same. He told them how he once caught a big snake alive with his hands and wrung it until it was dead, and then he put it inside his bag; but when he reached home he found a dead squirrel instead of the snake. They shouted and exclaimed, and laughed. They advised him to stop misusing the sweet voice which his chi had given him.

Joe whispered with Obieke. Then he clapped his hands. The noises diminished.

'May everyone here live very long.'

'And you too,' they answered.

'The night is far spent and I must say a word or two now in case any of you want to go away. I'm glad you were able

73

to come. I considered I ought to invite you to enjoy the moonlight with me. . . . E-e-e-e, I would like to take the opportunity to let you know what has been in my mind for some time now. I propose to start building my permanent residence. . . . May everybody live long.'

'And you too.'

There was some subdued and disorderly talking. Then someone spoke out:

'We've heard you, brother. And your words are sweet to our ears. But tell us, please, would you like us to tread the earth for mud?'

'No, no!' Uzondu said. 'He means to build a pan-roof house.'

They hushed him. And his brother Amaechina frowned and groaned in anger.

'Come out plain,' the speaker continued. 'When night has fallen on a discussion proverbs must be avoided.'

'Uzondu has already said it for me,' Joe said. 'It will be of stone walls and pan roof.'

'Gbam-gbam then?'

'Yes.'

'Did he say it's the sheets which they strike with some metal?' asked Ikeli.

'Yes,' they replied together.

'The one that knows no age, rain, or sun?'

'That's it.'

Nwokeji leapt up. 'Ta nma nma nu!'

'Yoh!'

'Louder. Nma nma nu!'

'Yoh!'

'Loudest now. Nma nma nu!'

'Yoh!'

'May the best of everything be found in our family.'

'Ofo!'

'So gbam gbam is about to reach Udemezue's family,' remarked another.

'It will be the fifth in Umudiobia, and the very first in our village.'

'Okafo, hear this from your bed!'

'Your father's obi is intact,' Ikeli said. 'But this other thing!'

'She'll be all right,' said they together in an undertone of sympathy.

'What I'll require is assistance in clearing and levelling the site, and also in collecting stone for the walls,' Joe cut in abruptly.

'We'll help in any way we can. Umudiobia still has a countless population and can carry all the stone in this world,' they answered.

All this time Willie had been listening; he had not said a single word. He was ill—he had a splitting head; but that was not the only reason. Obieke, his elder brother, had become seriously annoyed with him that evening and called him names the ear should not hear. Obieke called him a worthless creature and a disaster, in addition to other things. The words wounded Willie's heart, just as they were meant to.

And now, Willie suddenly revived and began to preach liberation. He approached the subject from the angle of Hitler vanquishing the oppressor and driving him away from the colonies. But the speech jarred on his listeners' nerves. Was Hitler not the one who was out to destroy the world? asked they, referring to the information they had recently received from the District Officer's agents. What had put such ideas into Willie's head? When he attempted to speak again they hushed him, and some advised him to resume his brooding instead of saying such horrible things.

Then Joe brought one more jar of wine. At the sight of

that, Uzondu sprang up from his seat, beamed, beckoned. He should bring the thing close to his legs, Uzondu requested.

'Rather than leave it in the container—' called someone.

'—let it remain in the stomach,' Uzondu interposed.

The rest burst into laughter. Even Willie laughed, in spite of the drumming that was going on inside his head.

*

Joe was talking with Obieke when Adagu came in the following morning.

'Father, tell me, is it true?' asked she as soon as she was seated.

'What?'

'That you intend to build a pan-roof house.'

'Is that why you've come all the way? How did you get to hear about it?'

'Please tell me.'

'Yes, it's true,' Joe said. 'In fact, Obieke and I were just wondering when we should invite the umuada and tell them about it.'

She ran out.

'My father's family may the very best be found in it. Daughter of Amanze, your chi is good!' She touched her chest. 'Son of Okafo, your chi is awake. . . . ' The song was flat and unrhythmic. But it served her purpose: she was singing out her heart. Then she began to dance. She danced with her feet, her fingers and her eyes. And from inside the house, Joe and Obieke watched.

'Midday lunatic, that's enough now,' Obieke said.

She ran forward again, lurched. She turned and ran once more, this time towards the house. A few feet from the entrance door, she dodged, halted.

'Akuka, come in please,' said Obieke. Akuka was a lunatic well-known throughout Umudiobia for the speed with which she chased invisible shapes.

When in the end Adagu returned into the house they began to fix the day on which the umuada were to be invited. Tentatively, they agreed it would be three oye markets from then.

'They will also like to hear when they come that you've decided to marry a second wife,' she said. Her tone suggested they had been discussing that subject among themselves.

Joe recoiled momentarily. Then he attempted, unsuccessfully, to smile. A vein stood out on his forehead.

Nobody spoke for some time.

'Did I annoy you?'

He would not reply. It was Obieke who spoke. 'You women! So you think he would wait for you to advise him before he marries a second wife?' Obieke said, diplomatically.

'I didn't mean to annoy you, Father.' She rose. 'We'll come on the date fixed, all of us. And we shall sing. For the news is a happy one.'

As she went away she wondered within herself how she could approach the question next time. How could she get him to marry a second wife?

*

They assembled at nightfall on the appointed day. All of them had their clappers. One brought a big metal gong, another a music-pot.

They drank two big jars of wine. Then they began to sing, beating the clappers in accompaniment. But the performance was yet intermittent: they sang and clapped for some time, then drank; and so on. None danced. What mattered at this stage was that they should make their presence felt; they should announce to Umudiobia that they were free-born, and that they were proud of the family. Let everybody realize that they were assembled in their own brother's house. And let the jealous choke with anger. What one had received from one's chi only a fool would grudge. . . . Such things did the umuada say in song.

Anna brought a pot of yam stewed with fish and a basin of rice. Then she brought another basin, containing a waist of goat. They clapped their hands and cried 'kili kilio. . . . Yoh!' Their brother was a very wise man, they commented. In spite of his many years abroad he still recognized the customs of the land; he still remembered that the waist of an animal was for the daughters of the family.

They then got down to business. They shared the yam first, each one eating her own share by hand. Next, they shared out the rice on cocoyam and banana leaves, and finally the meat. A few ate a part of their shares and made a parcel of the remainder. The rest parcelled up the whole portion: they would eat it at home with their children. But not the meat, of course. The meat was strictly for their husbands, or their husbands' fathers.

Then Joe told them about the proposed building. As was his habit, he spoke for a short time—in fact less than ten minutes. 'May everyone of you live long!' he ended, just as he had begun. And they answered in a chorus: 'And you too!'

'Kili kili kilio!' called a tall, energetic one amongst them, and they answered 'Yoh!' three times.

'Who spoke?'

'We spoke.'

'Your name?'

'Udemezue's daughters.'

'Which Udemezue?'

'The one that was great.'

'Kilio!'

'Yoh!'

'Gome!' the gong boomed in support.

There was a brief pause. 'We've heard you, our brother,' the tall one went on. 'We'll now whisper among ourselves. We will give our reply as soon as we are ready.'

It took them a good thirty minutes.

'We'll tell you our feeling in plain language;' said she now. 'First, we thank you for the food and the drink— you and your wife. We thank you too for the news that has come from your lips. In point of fact, we've all heard the men mumbling to themselves, and we thought they wanted to keep us in the dark. We're now reassured.' She paused. They asked her to go ahead, saying her mouth was sweet. 'We'll help in any way we can. However, we'll go home first and tell those to whom we belong—those to whom you gave your sisters.'

Joe thanked them and returned to the sitting-room where Anna was. From there they watched.

The gong droned and the pot boomed. The umuada picked up the clappers. They began to clap, the right on the left. It took little time to establish the rhythm—fast and yet strict, with regular syncopations. Kpam kpam kpam kpa-kpam kpam kpa-kpam. . . .

And then the soloist began to sing and everyone to dance, one after the other. The dancer would continue until the singer's voice had fallen, and there would be an interval during which the music continued. And then, the singer would burst out again, and another would come out to dance.

If she was young and stray the dancer would stamp hard; if she was old she just swayed, or shuffled, or shook her head.

They had gone on for a fairly long time, yet the rhythm still sounded deep and rich. Adagu put down her clappers, rose and went inside the house. Another, her fellow-conspirator, began to clear the dancing space. And then, the moon appeared in the sky, at long last, as if she had just been persuaded to grace the occasion with her queenly presence.

Soon they saw Adagu pulling Anna out of the house and on towards the dancing space. Anna was smiling bashfully. Adagu held her firmly and dragged her on and on, into the space.

'Go on, stand there and let's watch you,' Adagu said, then withdrew and re-joined the party. She picked up her clappers.

The soloist sang: 'Let's see her move her legs.'

A voice answered: 'That's what we're waiting to see.'

'Or is she a stone that can't move at all?'

They all answered: 'That's what we're waiting to see.'

'But what am I saying? She's beginning to tread!'

'That's what we're awaiting. . . .'

'She's doing it well, our good wife is.'

'That's what we're awaiting. . . .' They beat their clappers louder.

'Fancy that, she dances with such finesse. . . . See how she smiles and sways and balances. . . . But does she only know how to shuffle. . . . She seems to have no energy in her! . . . kpam kpam kpam kpa-kpam kpam kpa-kpam. . . .'

Anna lost all inhibition. The smile vanished from her face. She stamped hard and steadily, and beads of perspiration covered her face. There was no more singing now.

Instead, they hummed in unison, giving out deep, vigorous, throbbing rhythm.

'I can easily recognize the raffia palm,' the soloist sang again. And she was right. Like that tree which pours out its life together with its wine, Anna had poured out all the energy in her. Her steps were now unsteady and she danced out of beat. Mercifully, they stopped clapping. They yelled in applause. Then Joe dashed out from the house into the dancing space. He stuck a shilling on Anna's face. Chinwe came out too, but she had no money, so she merely hugged Mamma and screamed in praise. Many of the women rummaged hurriedly in their bags and rushed forward, and stuck cowrie shells on her face.

The confusion was hardly over when Uzondu came in. All attention turned to him. They called him some of his more popular nicknames, one of which was The Handwork of an Amateur Taxidermist.

Ten

THE SITE ON which the house was to be built was only a hundred yards, or even less, away from the old compound. It took the kinsmen two days to clear the area, and another seven to stump and level it. And all that cost Joe just a meal and some jars of palm wine, each day. Then they fixed a day for carrying stone. Four markets from then, they said. They would go to Ugwuchukwu, the rocky hill in Nade.

The hill had once been the abode of the gods. That was why it was still called Ugwuchukwu—Gods' Hill. The popular belief was that the gods deserted it on that day when bald-headed Francis Osita arrived from Ania along the river to begin a church in Nade. Neither the hill nor the stone belonged to anybody in particular now. However, that did not mean that anyone, even strangers, had free access to it. The kinsmen therefore advised Joe to go to Nade first and obtain the rulers' permission to use the quarry. He should kneel before the rulers and greet them like a son. He was after all the son of a daughter of the soil. No normal person would deny such a favour to a sister's son.

The rulers were exceedingly delighted to receive him— a son of a daughter dearer to the heart than even one's own child! But what delighted their hearts most was the big he-goat he brought to them as a present, and the way he prostrated before them and called them Fathers. Here was a man who had been to places, and even lived with the white man, they remarked; and yet he still remembered he should kneel down and greet them. But they were not surprised: Chiaku was his mother, and his father Okafo used to be a good man. Let him collect as much stone as he pleased. But why shouldn't he come and build the house in Nade instead of Umudiobia. After all, it was Nade that had brought him up!

'About that, don't we say in proverb that nobody ever leaves his father's ama for his mother's?' he replied.

'That's a true word, my son,' they echoed heartily.

They gave him some presents. One gave him a fowl and another gave him a coconut. Another waved at the universe and asked him to please himself.

'Your wife, how many has she now?'

He smiled weakly. 'Not yet.'

'And what have you been waiting for.'

He did not reply. He hurried away.

Preparations began in earnest as soon as it was known that Nade had allowed free access to the quarry. The umuada met again, this time in Nwokeji's obi, and on their own accord. They agreed that they must make their own contribution. Being women, they could not carry stone. Instead they would cook food for the men who would carry. They would send a team of six each morning to cook in their brother's house. And they would bring the cassava themselves. And their husbands, in keeping with custom, would come and pound the cassava they boiled. It was just one of the duties a son-in-law, if he was good and fit, owed to the wife's family—to pound boiled cassava on ceremonial occasions. And of course nobody who called himself a man would come empty-handed to pound cassava: the husbands would bring jars of wine. With the wine their brother would entertain the workers.

The following day they sent four representatives to

tell Joe and Obieke about the decision.

As the news spread, many offered to assist. Some were individuals; some were groups. They were mostly those to whom Joe had done one favour or another since his return. They wanted to use this opportunity to show their gratitude. They were all set, waiting for the Monday morning on which the work would start. Then, on the evening of the preceding Sunday, something happened.

*

Daylight was fast contracting into darkness. It was the hour when the tapper, perched on a tree, sees little but hears afar.

'Di di di. . .' tom-tom beats announced frantically. The message was for every adult male in Umudiobia. It came from the paramount chief's palace. Tax officials would be around in the morning, for a raid. The officials had just visited Nade; they would take Umudiobia next. Let everybody hide his property and make himself scarce for days. So the tom-tom warned.

Many years back, an order had come from the District Commissioner, now called simple District Officer, through his barefoot court messengers, that every adult male should pay a hundred and eighty heads of cowrie, which was sixpence, each year. Chief Nwigbo, the then paramount chief of Umudiobia, had replied:

'Friends, go and tell your white man that Umudiobia will not pay even a single cowrie shell. Tell him that's what I, Odezuluigbo of Umudiobia whose name rings all over Ibo land, have said.'

Then the officials began to explain, with unusual patience and humility. The monies so realized would be used in developing Umudiobia and other towns around. Roads

84

would be built, so also schools and hospitals. The money would not actually go into the white man's pocket but would be locked up in the Commissioner's safe at Ossa, and used as the need would arise, and accounted for in the end. But the promises, more exaggerated than even an election manifesto, failed to move the chief. The idea of paying money to an outside authority was to him phoney and insulting. Did they mean to say that the fore-fathers did not get on well? And did the fore-fathers pay money to any white man? the Odezuluigbo railed.

Then the officials reverted to type. 'Look here, Chief,' their leader warned, irritably. 'This is the white man's word and therefore must be obeyed. We've respected you as much as we possibly could, but you don't seem to appreciate. Either you get your people to pay or you will no longer be chief and in addition go to jail for as many years as there are grains on a big cob of maize!'

The experiences of other chiefs had taught the Odezuluigbo that it was dangerous to ignore an ultimation from court messengers, or to allow them to depart without gifts. Chief Ofoma of Obizi was an example. Ofoma, who was still in jail, had tried to obstruct a rather unimpressive court messenger that came into Obizi to serve a summons. That was only the year before! And so, having put up a show of resistance, the Odezuluigbo yielded. Not only that, he placated the court messengers with a big he-goat and ten shapely yams; he also supplied carriers to take those from Umudiobia to Ossa on a hill.

In the first two years the amount realized from the tax was far below what the District Commissioner had expected. In fact, it was only fifteen pounds and a few shillings. The Commissioner therefore decided that the exact number of taxable males should be shown, village by village. The idea was that from the figures, it would be easy to say how much money was expected from each village. And the village-head would be required to pay in that amount to the tax officials.

The idea revolted the people. 'The white man wants to count our heads, does he?' they exclaimed. That was abomination. As if they were cattle! It would never happen.... So they said. But none would have dared do so in the presence of the District Commissioner, Arthur Bowles, the strapping one who often used his fists to ram into people's heads what he said with his mouth. One thing, however, they were able to do. Each village submitted about a third of their actual number. They then shared the total assessment among themselves. The result was that each paid less than a third of a hundred and eighty heads of cowrie shells.

But soon, the officials discovered the trick, and devised their own answer to it. Since only those people were supposed to exist whose names were on the tax list, then one was at liberty to do anything to any others who might be found in the villages. Indeed one could even confiscate and sell such people's property, thought the officials. There was no fear about the evaders coming to Ossa to lodge a complaint, since they were not supposed to exist; and besides by complaining, they would expose the village-heads too, and in fact expose the entire town.

The officials made a good haul in the first year. But in the second year they were greatly disappointed. For the town, wiser now, took adequate precaution. Umudiobia decided to make themselves scarce during the raids, except the ones that had tax-receipts. They also took their most valuable belongings into the forests and covered up all foot-prints and tell-tale signs. Some handed over their property to the ones that had tax-receipts. The trick had worked quite satisfactorily for years now, although the officials would always manage to make a few arrests or to confiscate some property which their owners later redeemed with money. The tom-tom was now warning them to go far into the heart of the forests. 'Go right inside and take what you ought to take. . . . Let the white man and his servants come and arrest their mothers. . . . Umudi-obia of ten villages and two, the message is for you.'

The night was windless and sultry. Everybody thought that rain was about to fall. Yet up to midnight not a single drop had fallen—only frequent rumblings and flashes in the sky. It was at second cock-crow that the rain came. It poured with fury as if it was avenging the drought of the past few weeks. And it continued well into mid-morning.

Most people believed that the officials would not come again. Joe, too, thought so. But at mid-morning, somebody ran in.

'Just from Ume's house—Ume who is the head of our village. He wants you at once,' the man panted out.

'Anything wrong?' asked Joe.

He replied in a whisper: 'Court messengers. They've come on a tax raid.'

He was sure it had something to do with money, said Joe to himself as he rode to the village-head's compound. He was once an employee of Government. He knew the tricks of such men. They made money out of every situation.

That was why he quarrelled with many while he was at Abagwa. People called him a wicked man; others said he was foolish. Just because he refused to accept what they euphemistically called Reward. 'Our people's custom is that a visitor must be entertained.' That was what Jerry, himself a Forest Guard too, used to say. 'And why should that custom not apply to us when we visit people and places?' Jerry was perhaps the most corrupt of all the officials at Abagwa. Jerry wouldn't even take out the stamp from his pocket unless you had paid money. But that wasn't the whole story. All the money went to women. He had many concubines. But thinking about it, what did people do with the money they received? . . .

He was indeed very glad; he never yielded to the temptation, reflected Joe. And he had no remorse about what he once did to Ephraim. Ephraim insisted on bribing him, in spite of all the time he took to advise him.

The story was quite straightforward. Ephraim wanted to fell without a permit and saw some irokos. 'It's impossible,' Joe had said outright, and then began to explain. Nobody could fell iroko without the District Officer's permission. There was fear that the trees would be exhausted within a few years unless some control was imposed; that was why there was such restriction. Then he advised Ephraim to apply for the permit. This happened at Obali, some ten miles away from Abagwa.

When he went to the place again a few days later, Ephraim had already felled four trees. To make matters worse, Ephraim came to him with some money, a bottle of gin, and a young girl. The fool, he thought all government employees were the same! But he learnt his lesson in the end: the magistrate sentenced him to one year and six months. And people said things: Joe was wicked; Ephraim would send thunder to strike him; and so on and so forth. But he merely laughed. He had been waiting for the thunder since then. . . .

He was now only a short distance from the village-head's compound. He went into a neighbour's house. There he left his bicycle and he put out his shirt. He wore only brown shorts and a grey sleeveless singlet, which was simple enough and would not attract undue attention. Then he walked over to the compound.

Inside the village-head's obi one of the officials sat

smoking a cigarette, which readily suggested that he was the leader. Joe went in straight to meet him.

'Good day,' he greeted.

The official surveyed him haughtily and in silence.

'You've come from Ossa, I hear.'

'Your tax-receipt first.'

Joe produced the pink paper.

'You are not a village-head or a chief, are you?'

'No, but why do you ask?'

'Because you look so neat and prosperous, but more, so that you'll be arrested for hiding tax-evaders.'

'I see.'

'You behave in an arrogant manner. Who are you?'

Joe did not reply.

And at this point Ume, the village-head, came out from the dwelling house which was farther in. He walked dreamily and he looked sombre, wretched. Somebody, a stranger, was following behind him. The man was an official. The village-head was already under arrest.

'Come and whisper with me,' he said wearily to Joe.

They conferred for a few moments. Then, returning, Joe said to the officials:

'He has told me about your talk with him. There won't be any problem about it, we'll give you the fifteen you've asked for.'

'Rich man!' replied the leader, sarcastically.

'We don't want this case to get to Ossa.'

'It will depend on you people,' his Assistant said.

'I know. We'll see you before you leave. Let me go to my house and search.'

'If you keep us busy here we can wait till you return.'

'We are not children. We won't let you stay without food and drinks.'

'Is that all your people can afford? Didn't I hear that

your town has many beautiful creatures?'

'Look round then and let's see if there are any particular ones—'

'Man, it seems you understand the language of officials,' said the leader with some thrill.

'Perhaps I do.' He frowned. 'Do you know Mr Ifeka?'

'Which one?'

'The District Clerk at Ossa? His first name is Raymond.'

'You know him, do you?'

'Yes, we are friends—good ones.' He stepped forward aggressively.

They both swallowed and moved sideways, apart.

'I was in school with him.'

'True!' gasped the two together.

Silence fell.

'Next time I go to Ossa I'll tell him how you do your work. I'll tell him that you go to places and demand bribe,' Joe shouted. 'I'll tell him all the crimes you've been committing. And thank God, he's not a corrupt man himself. . . .'

They really shook with fear. They knew the District Clerk was a very strict man when it came to that. Then the leader began to plead, in the name of his three wives and twelve children, his old father and his late brother's children.

They returned to Ossa that day without any tax-evaders or village-head, and without bribe money. Instead, they were glad that Joe wasn't going to report to the District Clerk who was their master—at least Joe had promised so. And the news soon spread all over the village. Joseph Okafo had sent away the wicked court messengers from the town. He had done what nobody ever did. They would show him how grateful they were for that.

That evening the village tom-tom summoned all the family heads. They assembled in the morning, after breakfast. They decided they should express their gratitude in a practical way. Every adult male in the village should do a trip to Nade to bring stone for the new house. Each family was to see that the decision was enforced. Masquerades would be asked to do the usual thing, which was to loot offenders' houses, unless such offenders were Christians. As for the latter, one could only hope that they would all turn up to help their member.

And indeed, there were hardly any defaulters, apart from members of rival sects in whose case nothing could be done. Day in day out, they went to Nade in groups and singles. And people wondered what type of building it was going to be for which the whole village had turned out, in addition other groups. A few weeks after, there were many large heaps of stone at the site, sufficient, as some said, to give a set of potstands to every house-wife in Umudiobia of ten villages and two.

Eleven

'WILL IT BEGIN to sing if you bring this down?' Obiakizu asked.

'Bring what down?' asked Joe in reply.

There was a gramophone on the table in front of them. Obiakizu pointed at the open lid and said: 'This.'

'No.' He inserted the winding rod.

'He-i!'

'What is it now?'

'Look at that dog there,' said he and touched the badge, the trade-mark, which was pasted on the interior side of the lid. 'Is it the one that sings?'

With them in the house was a small group of six, among whom were Obieke and Uzondu. These broke into laughter.

'Dogs bark; they don't sing,' Uzondu said, and drawing the boy towards him, he began to whisper into his right ear.

'It's a lie!' Obiakizu suddenly cried.

'It's true!' Uzondu insisted.

'It's a lie, it's a lie!'

'It's true; it's true!'

'I'll ask him.'

'Go on.'

'Is it true that there are four hundred small children inside the thing?' Obiakizu asked.

'Who said so?' replied Joe.

'Uzondu. He says it's they who sing.'

'It's true,' answered Uzondu himself. 'Watch closely when the thing begins to sing and you'll see the children hopping about.'

'It's a lie.' He touched the turn-table slyly and withdrew his hand immediately, as if from fire.

'Don't do that again!' Joe objected seriously. 'If you do, I'll put it back inside the room.'

The warning kept him quiet and steady. For the past four days he had been begging Joe to play the gramophone for him. He had even gone so far as to promise he would fetch a pot of water each day for the rest of his life. Today, he had run over to the house first thing in the morning; and he came close to tears when Joe tried to make the usual excuses.

Just as the needle was coming down on the record, a voice cried outside the yard. They listened in silence.

'Ko-ko-koi!' the voice cried again.

'Everybody to his own!' another said.

'That was Adagu's voice,' Obieke said.

Adagu danced in, followed by Ugoada, also a daughter of the extended family.

'My good father, you didn't offend against custom!' Adagu exclaimed. 'And you didn't offend the gods!'

'Get on with it, Sister, your voice is good,' the other said.

Adagu stretched out her hands and spread out her palms, like one begging for alms. She reared, tip-toed forward, lurched. Then she stepped backward. She halted, threw her legs apart and expanded her chest. They came out from the house and watched.

'Our sister, you behave as if Akuka had asked you to deputize for her today,' Uzondu said.

'This isn't a day for fat creatures,' she replied, staring

93

at the sky, and stamped her right foot on the ground. She moved a few paces forward and stamped again. Then she began singing, once more in praise of her late father, Amanze.

They asked Ugoada what it was all about. Ugoada began to explain. They went to see Unebo about Ebenma's new child, she said, Unebo was the seer and Ebenma was Nwokeji's second wife. Could any of them guess what Unebo told them?

'No, no, no! Don't tell them anything yet!' Adagu cried and waved her hand in objection, having just concluded one more song, spontaneously composed. 'Let them give us something first. Obieke,' said she, gazing steadily at her half-brother, 'give us something at once.'

Joe sighed and laughed dully. 'You pagans do very funny things,' he said. But they ignored him—all of them. Ugoada went on with her story. The child, was none other than Amanze. Amanze had all these years refused to be re-incarnated; he was waiting to return as Joe's child. That was what Unebo had told them. Having disagreed with his nephew in his first life, Amanze had been anxious to make amends. And what better amends could he have made than to be reincarnated in his nephew's family? But after he had waited for so long a time, he decided to go into another family.

'We had thought he offended the gods,' Adagu now said, beaming and sweating. 'We thought that was why he could not be re-incarnated. We didn't know that he was waiting for his own.' She dashed forward, furiously, towards Obieke. She held him on the shoulders and looked straight into his face. 'Go on now, I want my reward for this. I it was who got the message from the seer.'

'Two of us, Sister,' Ugoada corrected promptly, in the interest of fair-play. Then Obieke invited them both to come over to his house later in the day.

An excited argument soon developed. Joe started it. He declared that there was no such thing as reincarnation. They retorted that the Christians were certainly big fools when it came to such matters. For what else did they think happened to the spirits of the righteous dead? How could families stay together if the dead fathers did not return in new bodies? And were there not many cases in which the dead had returned to life with the same scars they had in their earlier existence? What else could explain the fact that Obiakizu was so attached to him, other than that they were father and son? .... They spoke simultaneously and Joe found their voices overwhelming. He capitulated and began to smile.

All this time, Obiakizu had been wriggling and scratching his stomach impatiently. When he heard his name mentioned he issued a stern warning. Then he moved closer still, towards the gramophone.

'Make it sing now,' he pleaded.

Joe lifted the sound-box.

'Yes, it will soon begin,' said he authoritatively. 'Please let nobody talk again.'

The voices died down. They watched.

The arm swung lamely, like the boneless python. The spring began to unwind, and the turn-table began to rotate. Then the needle came down on the outer edge of the record. It slipped on with a harsh, metallic sound. A moment later, it entered the groove. A male voice burst out, replacing the scratching sound.

The voice sang. 'Most beautiful Helen, you must be having a wonderful time!' it said. 'Who is the man?' Then it proceeded to lament her absence, pledging unflinching fidelity, love and affection. When it stopped they all jeered. The men said that the singer was unfit to be a man; that the woman, Helen, must have emptied something into his soup. The women concurred but declared that only wives like Helen could teach most men the much-needed lesson.

*

'What is it a proverb says?' asked Adagu and replied: 'The child who watches a performing monkey runs the risk of missing the day's work. Let's not forget, sister, what has brought us here.'

'That's true, sister,' Ugoada replied.

The gramophone had played for some thirty minutes, one record after another, and they had even begun to dance. Obiakizu danced most and now perspiration covered his body. Uzondu rocked in his seat.

'Put that box aside, Father,' Adagu said. 'We want to have a word with you.'

'Hear her, she calls kramafunu a box,' Obiakizu derided, and laughed. Uzondu asked whether she knew what she was talking, to which she replied:

'Big Sack, that's all that interests you. We've been waiting to hear that you're getting ready to marry.'

'Marry? Not Uzondu!' said Uzondu. 'Do you know, I once decided to look for a wife.'

'In the land of fairies, I suppose.'

'And I did find one.'

'And where is she now?'

'I was coming to that. Yes, I found her. Then, one morning I set out to take a jar of rich palm-wine to my prospective father-in-law. And do you know what happened?'

'A bush fowl saw me and started to crow a warning. 'Woman is trouble, woman is trouble!' it said. Of course, I turned back. And I drank my wine when I reached home.'

Joe played four more records after that. Then Adagu

stood up and threatened seriously she would carry the gramophone to her husband's house.

He went out to the front yard with Adagu and Ugoada. He had a strange feeling that they were going to say something unpleasant, even jarring.

'Yes?' he said.

'Father, it's true we went to enquire about Ebenma's new child. But that's only part of our mission. The other is to give you a message from the umuada,' Adagu said.

There was a pause. 'Get on, please.'

Ugoada continued: 'They asked us to inform you that they'll come to see you on afo day after next, which is seven days from now.'

'All of them?'

'No, only six representatives, one from each branch of Udemezue's family.'

'Oh, good. I was afraid I would have to entertain a large number. What is it about, do you know?'

'Nothing serious,' said Adagu in a low, slow, thoughtful, voice. 'There's no need peering into a parcel when it's about to be opened, anyway. And remember to keep something for them.'

They went back to the house. Anna brought a pot of yam stewed with fish, but said it was for the two women only. However, immediately she had put it down, Uzondu began to advance at an impressive speed. The two stared at him fiercely.

He dipped his hand into the pot and lifted out a big piece, daring the women to abandon the food if they were really angry. In reply they called him a couple of nicknames. And while everybody, including Uzondu himself, was laughing, Adagu cleverly retrieved the pot. Then they retired to the back-yard, where they could eat the yam undisturbed.

Twelve

THE SUN had hardly risen when they began to assemble on the appointed day. Within a space of thirty minutes they had all arrived—the six of them. As soon as they had eaten kola the discussion started. Ugoada was their chief spokesman.

'Father, we here have come as representatives of the six obis in the family,' she said. 'And it was the umuada that sent us.'

'Hold on, please,' another interrupted. 'Where's Onna?'

'Anna, not Onna,' she corrected.

'I can call her anything I like. I don't go to church. Where is she? We don't want her to overhear.'

'She's at the backyard,' Joe said. 'She went back after greeting you.' Anna had actually gone back to cook breakfast for them.

'I should have asked her to mend my cloth for me while we're here!' said a humble-looking one among them and displayed the tear that ran some inches up from her left knee.

'True, Sister, you've need for such service,' Ugoada said. 'But that's not what we've come here for. At least you look better than Akuka.'

'But why shouldn't she be allowed to overhear?' shouted another. 'Let her come and listen while we speak. This obi must not be allowed to disappear.' She stared furiously into the air and she bit her lower lip. Her nickname was Warrior,—a tall, strong woman who in her younger days had wrestled and thrown many boys of her age—not just Uzondu. And she was bold and forthright in speech. In serious issues, Warrior had proved herself the glory of Udemezue's family. 'Why hide it from her?' she asked, after a tense pause.

Joe's first impulse was to rise and rail and order them out of the house. But he managed to control himself. He shifted uneasily in his seat. Then a strange smile furrowed his cheeks.

'Is that what you people have come for?' he asked.

'Definitely,' the warrior confirmed.

'Shut up, Sister,' Ugoada took over once more. 'We've come to talk with our brother. Nothing else.' She turned to him: 'Yes, we've come to talk like sisters to a brother, in a quiet and frank way.'

'Go on,' he said.

'You see, we've collected stone with which you'll build your house. And the site has been cleared and stamped. We hear the builders will start work any time from now.' She paused. 'It will be gbam gbam house for which we're all very happy. But have you considered who will live there when we're all dead? This is just one of the many questions that have been worrying our minds, day and night—even in our dreams.'

There was another interval. He stared at them, from one to another, in rebuke. But they were not moved.

'We've seen the wife you brought home. We were angry with you at the beginning for marrying a stranger; we no longer are. We think she's well-bred. And she's beautiful too. But then, what use is a kolanut tree if it fails to bear fruits?'

'If that's all you've come here for you had better go home

in time, before the day begins to get hot.'

'We'll go home quite all right, but not until we've finished saying what we have in mind,' Warrior replied.

'And what would happen if I should fail to listen to you any more?'

'Can you do such a thing to us who are Udemezue's daughters?' asked Adagu.

They told the story of a certain man who recently beat his wife until the teeth flew out of her mouth. Then they talked about some other things. Tempers went down and the heat cleared. Even Joe joined in, and a smooth, unconscious rhythm was established in the conversation.

Some thirty minutes passed.

'What we were saying, Father, was for your own good and that of the family,' Adagu reverted. 'Don't get annoyed with us.'

'Isn't it almost six years now since you were married?' asked Ugoada. 'And yet—'

'Of course we can't call her our wife yet,' Warrior said. 'Not until she's produced for us.'

'There are many unmarried women in Umudiobia,' said the one with a tear in her cloth. 'Beautiful ones and ugly ones; tall ones and short ones. You have the money and I don't see why you shouldn't marry up to seven. If you ask me I can arrange for that. Only, whoever you marry let her produce for us.'

'It's enough now, let us hear him speak. Father, we're waiting to have your reply?'

'Reply to what?' he asked.

'What we've said.'

'What do you think you've said?'

'We want you to marry another wife.'

He paused. 'Didn't I tell you people to go home if that

was the only thing you came here to discuss?'

'Father, listen,' Adagu pleaded.

'Shut up, you!' he demanded. 'I know it was you who organized them to come and say such things to me.'

Her silence confirmed this.

'There's nothing wrong in her bringing us to speak to you,' Ugoada interceded. 'It's for your own good after all.'

'So you people don't know that I'm a Christian?'

'We do indeed,' Adagu replied, in a ruffled tone. 'Just like Alisa of Amano village—he now calls himself Edward. His wife has seven daughters and not one single son, and yet he has refused to marry another. He's now on the brink of death. The very half-brother of his who is known to have poisoned him will inherit all his property when he dies! Church indeed!' she repeated, with bitter scorn. 'Daniel who is chief of Ujiji, isn't he a church man? Yet he married two other wives when he found that his first wife was not going to bear children. He has since left the church.'

'You may talk any nonsense you please,' he replied, and his legs began to quiver, and a big vein ran prominently down his forehead. 'I will not leave the church and will not marry a second wife. Go and tell those that sent you.'

'Then why not join the Opirichualili who marry as many wives as they can afford?' Ugoada suggested.

'That's true,' several voices said.

'I'm more worried about the whole thing than anybody else,' Adagu moaned, tearfully. 'Look at Obieke. He has lost his first wife who is Obiakizu's mother. Now he has three girls from Akueze—no boy at all. So Obiakizu is the only male. Willie is twenty-five and yet he's not talking about marriage. Therefore, in Okoli's family we have only—' She broke down and the tears came down in big drops. She sobbed. 'People will soon begin to say there's a curse in this family!' Adagu cried, and the others up-braided her.

'That's all very foolish,' he said. 'You've never considered that I would not have been so well off but for the church.'

'Your being well off! What could that mean when there's nobody to inherit your property?'

'Of course you are talking like a woman.'

Warrior intervened. 'Women indeed we are.' she said. 'We differ from the men in that we speak out our feeling without fear. You perhaps don't know that they feel as we do.'

'They told you?'

'Ask them.'

Ugoada tried another angle: 'The spirits of the righteous dead have been waiting to reincarnate in your own family.'

He laughed. 'Tell them to stay where they are.'

'Let's go away, he doesn't want to listen to our advice.'

'Yes, go away at once.'

'What shall we tell the umuada?'

'I've already told you, haven't I?'

'Is that—?'

He interrupted. 'Please go away at once and don't come here again to annoy me.'

'You didn't keep anything for us?'

'Go away!' he ordered, and stamped his right foot emphatically on the floor. 'Don't come to my house again, do you hear?'

They rose in anger and began to leave. A few feet from the entrance door, Adagu halted, turned to face him.

'Let me say it again and let nobody try to hush me this time,' she shouted. 'We don't regard her as a wife. How can we allow Okafo's obi to disappear when the gods were kind enough to bring you home.'

Her voice was inordinately loud and the words reached Anna's ears. She dropped the kitchen knife in her hand. She sat still for some time, staring into space. Then she sprang up.

She ran into her room, flung herself heavily on the bed and thrashed about. Then she broke into a cry—soft but deeply sad, and cursed in tears the day she came into the world. She moaned: 'God, why not give me just one, even if its birth would mean my own death? . . . Let me die immediately it's been delivered. . . . Let me die even while it's coming out. . . . Provided it lives. But please, please, don't leave me in my present state!'

Joe came in. He saw her lying in the bed with her hair dishevelled, like a madwoman. Chinwe was leaning against the bed, weeping. 'Please, Mamma, stop saying such things!' she pleaded. But Anna went on, almost delirious, crying more and more, louder and louder, just as she had on that morning, nearly six years back, when she had her first miscarriage—distraught, her plaits torn, and tears streaking her cheeks and her arms spread wide, as if in capitulation. Yet she was still beautiful.

'Anna!' He held her hands and drew her up to a sitting position. He stared steadily into her face.

He sat by her side and wiped the tears. 'Do you know what you've been saying? Why do you talk like that?'

She picked up a silken head-tie and tried to wipe her face with it. She dropped it and her body jerked. It seemed as if she was shaking herself into consciousness. Then she broke into laughter, hollow, mirthless laughter.

'Nobody is God after all!' Anna said, then crossed herself. . . . Once more it had ended in prayer.

Thirteen

He went to see Obieke the next day, in the morning.

'I hear our umuada visited you yesterday.' Obieke had anticipated him. 'What was it that they wanted? Money?'

'That would have been much better,' he replied. 'They came to advise me to marry another wife.'

'They did? But of course there's nothing they would not do, those women.'

'They talked a lot of rubbish. Especially Adagu—she annoyed me most. And the one whom they call Warrior.'

'Egodinobi is her name.'

'I hate her mouth.'

'That's their way, my brother. They behave as if they owe us some grudge for sending them away from the family, to their husbands'. We of course are used to their tongue. You too will get used to it one day.'

'I've warned them not to come near my house again.'

Obieke laughed. 'And you expect them to obey you, do you? No, my brother. How many times now have I asked Adagu in anger never to step into my yard again? But each time, she would come back the following day to clear my barn.' He raised his voice purposely. 'In spite of all Adagu does I like her for one thing: she's the only person who can talk to the evil thing I call my wife in the language she deserves.'

In the back yard Akueze grumbled and invited thunder

to come and split his skull.

Obieke said after some time: 'I was wondering, Father, why don't we begin to look for a doctor?'

'What for?'

'I mean for Anna. I am not happy about her state. Our people say that man must do something to help his chi. Let us do something—not necessarily because of what umuada have said.' He spoke in a gentle and persuasive tone.

'She was taking some treatment before we returned,' Joe replied. 'We decided she should give her body some rest; that was why she hasn't been taking anything for some time now.'

'That was wise. I think she could start again.'

'Do you know any good doctor around? Anna is anxious herself.'

'Why? Emenike Nwoye of Ozala is there.'

'Who is he?'

'You haven't heard about him?' Then he began to narrate some of the stories connected with the doctor.

*

At first Anna was happy when Joe told her they would go and see Emenike of Ozala. Her countenance dulled when he gave more details. For Emenike was a magician, exorcist, herbalist and gynaecologist, all in one. It was said that he studied for all that in India. And Emenike never made any attempt to disclaim the tribute, or to tell the world the truth, which was that he had been in Yorubaland all the years he was supposed to be practising in Asia. Emenike had returned to Ozala only a few years before, and since then his reputation had been growing steadily among the neighbours.

'Will that not be a sin?' she asked.

'I don't think so, unless we went for the other things.'
'Perhaps that's true.'
'Let's go and see first. If he starts something we don't like, then——We have our feet after all.'

Seven days later they went to Ozala with Obieke. Obieke had made a previous appointment; they were therefore sure they would meet the busy doctor at home.

When they had got to the beginning of the long, broad approach, they saw a tall upright pole on top of which hung a white piece of cloth. Joe and Anna almost developed cold feet. Then, a short distance further in, they saw a weather-beaten sign-board. The picture of a human skeleton occupied the left side of the board. The right side carried the inscription:

EMENIKE NWOYE

The Dokitor of Medesin
Curer of Woman Diziz——
Miscarriage of Pregnant
Impregnant to pregnant
Cut-cut and gonoria
Also India love medicine
Try and see

Directly behind the sign was the small hall that was the doctor's waiting room. When they entered they saw a small group of people sitting on mud benches which were built on to the walls. A woman was groaning in pain. Another was narrating, by way of a consolation, what wonders Emenike had done to her once in similar circumstances.

They sat down. Not long after, Emenike entered. He was a short, stout man, middle-aged, heavily bearded, his hair long and unkempt. He surveyed the crowd with professional detachment, and went away again, to his dwelling house. And from the house he sent for the patients.

Thirty minutes later, Joe, Anna and Obieke sat facing the doctor.

'You said you would bring your brother's wife. Is she the one?' he asked.

'She is,' Obieke replied. 'And this is my brother—the one who returned not long ago.'

'Welcome, friend.'

Joe thanked him.

'And missus, welcome.'

Anna merely shook her head. She was still feeling very uncomfortable.

Emenike shifted importantly in his seat. 'Now, tell me the trouble.'

Joe wanted to speak, but the doctor refused: 'Let her speak for herself.'

Anna spoke slowly and disjointedly. It was four months after their wedding when it happened. . . . She had treatment. . . . The pain had long stopped. . . .

'You're sure about the pain?'

'Yes.'

'Do you drink gin?'

'No.'

'Beer?'

'No.'

'Whisky?'

'No.'

'Tea?'

'Yes.'

He made a wry face.

'What other things do you eat?'

She enumerated as many things as she could remember. When she mentioned fruits the doctor smiled and shook his head.

'You need to be more careful about your diet, missus,' he said. 'Fruits, especially oranges, set the stomach dancing. And avoid anything hot. Avoid milk. In short, white man's food. Eat plenty of cassava food, for it keeps the stomach steady, which is good for the womb.'

His tone changed. He spoke as if he was reciting a prayer. 'I am only a servant of the Gods. I will not say that it must happen, but, the gods willing, I am confident I shall succeed. One thing I know for certain is that I've dealt with such cases. Not once, not twice, but many many times. Anyway, let's pray to the gods.'

'Thank you, you've spoken well,' Joe acknowledged.

'Don't thank me yet. One of these days perhaps, you'll invite me to your house to see something that cries in its cot. Then will I receive your thanks with joy.'

'May it be so!' Obieke prayed.

A smile appeared on the doctor's face. 'And also, I'll ask you for a fat goat.'

'That won't be a problem,' Anna replied. She had at last begun to feel comfortable.

Then Emenike proceeded to state the fee. Five pounds, he said. But he was not going to demand all at the same time. He would take half the amount to start with, and the balance could be paid any time within three moons. If that was acceptable to them, he would start treatment as soon as possible.

They did not haggle, simply because Emenike did not allow that. However, they managed to persuade him to knock off a few shillings.

'We'll come back tomorrow morning with the first instalment,' Joe promised.

'I'll expect you. And I'll start the treatment right away. But don't come empty-handed as you did today. Bring me a jar of palm-wine or you'll pay a shilling in lieu.'

*

They set out the following morning with two jars of wine, as well as half the fee. They were anxious to please; and besides, he had impressed them very much the day before. They entered the house with confidence and sat down with cheerful faces.

The doctor emptied one of the jars into an empty calabash pot and put the pot away, for his personal use. They drank part of the other jar; then he emptied the remainder into another pot and put that aside, too. Then he went inside the room where he stored the herbs and shrubs.

He returned after about ten minutes. He brought with him a small earthen pot and a packet done up with dry banana leaf. He sat down, put the pot and the packet on the floor close to his feet.

'The money.'

Joe took it out from his pocket, counted, paid. Emenike counted, nodded.

'A hand shake,' said he and stretched out his hand to Anna. Anna hesitated; then she moved forward and shook.

Next, he lifted the pot into his left palm. He dipped a finger inside, touched the finger to his tongue. 'You will fill this with water up to the neck.' He handed the pot over to Anna. 'Drink a cupful three times each day, and re-fill it from time to time. Always shake the pot before you pour out to drink.'

He untied the packet and put some of the contents into an empty beer bottle. 'This, you will pour palm wine into the bottle on the seventh day. Drink half a cup before you eat breakfast each day, from then onwards. Add wine from time to time. After four weeks you must empty the bottle again and re-fill with half of what is left in this packet. Do the same thing again after another four weeks.'

He went in again.

'This,' said the doctor a few minutes later, and held up a tiny leather belt, 'is to be worn round the waist. Its own work is to keep off the evil spirits which destroy the seeds of life.'

'What?' Joe protested. Anna cried: 'Let's go away!' Obieke remained cautiously silent. The doctor held the belt suspended in his hand.

'What is wrong?' asked he, embarrassed.

'If you have no other medicine for us we better go away. We won't take that one,' Joe replied.

'Why?'

'Because it's a charm.'

He grunted. 'So you won't take it?'

'No!' Anna snapped, her face screwed up.

'We won't even touch it,' Joe added.

'Just as you wish. But don't blame me if you fail to obtain the result you expect.'

'Yes, let it be so,' she retorted.

'You may wish to know that there are other Christians like you who have accepted it gladly,' said Emenike Nwoye angrily. 'I can name three at least at Umubiobia from where you've come. Even the headmaster himself. I hear his wife is already delivered.

Joe and Anna exchanged shocked glances.

'Why not try it?' Obieke suggested.

'Try what? Anna, let's go.'

They went out without even the pot or the bottle.

It was Obieke who brought these home.

*

The next morning, Anna went to see the headmaster's wife. They had never been very good friends, and so it was strange for Anna to visit her so early in the day.

'We went to Ozala yesterday,' Anna said.

'What for?'

'To see Emenike.'

'Did you? I used to go there myself.'

'So he told us.'

'It was he who made me succeed,' she said. 'Do you know, I had almost given up hope. That was after my second child—we had none again for four good years. Then somebody told us about Emenike. We had just come here on transfer then. It took him only three months. What type of medicine did he give you?'

Anna described it.

'He didn't give you a leather belt for your waist?'

'No,' she said harshly.

'Then he didn't give you all you require. You must ask him for it when next you go there.'

She shrugged. 'I won't touch it. He wanted to give it to us but we told him it's a charm. It's sin.'

'Sin? I don't think so. It's just medicine. Even Teacher says there's nothing sinful about it.'

'Did he?'

'Ask him.'

Some time passed.

'But don't you think people would have been scandalized if they had seen you wearing it?'

'That would have been the sinful part.' She began to smile; which Anna did not understand.

'How?'

'Because nobody other than your own husband should see your waist.' She laughed.

Anna shrugged once more, rose, and went away.

She told Joe all that had passed as soon as she reached home.

Fourteen

THEY WERE BOTH confused for the headmaster looked indeed a devout Christian. He had holy pictures in his house and a crucifix hung on the wall of his sitting room, directly opposite the entrance door. His wife was the chairman of several church women's organizations in Umudiobia. How then could he be wrong? Perhaps there was nothing sinful about a leather belt.

'No, I'm sure the First Commandment forbids it!' Joe suddenly declared, speaking from the depth of his conscience.

'I thought it did—not until I went to see her,' she said.

'Remember what the catechism says. 'The First Commandment forbids divination, pagan sacrifices, charms. . . .' That belt is a charm.'

'Let's not accept it then. I'm serious.'

Soon after, she retired to bed.

Joe was now alone in the sitting-room. He was thinking. A leather belt round the waist to keep off evil spirits! There was no doubt about it; it was charm. He should have nothing to do with it.

His mind wandered. He thought about his experiences at Abagwa when he was a Forest Guard. There, nearly everybody who worked for Government had charms on his body or in his house. Some did that for protection; some to secure advance in rank; some for both. Yet they all still answered their Christian names. Aaron, the police sergeant, was an example. Aaron had a wicker basket mounted on three stands in front his house. Once each week he would kill a cock and sprinkle the blood and pluck off some of the feathers, into the basket. But the worst was Samuel Ikedi, the Native Court Clerk, popularly known as Sam the Great. All sorts of things were to be found in Sam's house— red marks on walls, ceramic moulds, animal skins, leather balls, pots and baskets with curious contents, plumes and feathers. Samuel would start each day by firing a gun at the rising sun; then he would bite his right forefinger and flick it hard in a painful gesture, and mutter words of abuse to all his enemies in this world.

Sam kept a big, rectangular, open-topped wooden box at the corner of the sitting-room of his house. Inside, clay miniatures of giants stood and gaped with a sheepish complacency at a small figure; green leaves were scattered over the base and the sides. It was said that his priest-doctor was out to endow him, a small, lean man, with the strength to command his subordinates as well as the power to control the white man's will. And to most, it seemed that the priest-doctor did accomplish the aim, for Sam was soon the most feared man in Abagwa. The District Officer himself, Mr Shanks, was known to have once said that without him it would have been very difficult, if not impossible, to tame the natives of Abagwa.

Once Sam had the occasion to prove to the world how strong he really was. That was when he dealt with Mr Jumbo, his immediate runner-up at Abagwa. Jumbo was aspiring to the master's position and had tried both intrigue and blackmail. When he found that he could not succeed in that way, he had recourse to charms. Jumbo paid ten pounds to the priest-doctor to strike Sam with white disease, a disease of the worst type which eats away the limbs and bites through the nose. So the story went.

Sam came to learn about it. 'I whom they call Sam the Great!' he cried out, and shrugged, and struck his breast three times. 'I to whom dibias make obeisance! I before whom chiefs have bowed! This small fly will soon find itself drowning in a pot of red palm-oil.' Sam said all this in his office and many people, including Jumbo himself, heard him. And he did not stop there; he summoned Jumbo to his table, issued a stern warning, and demanded atonement. But Jumbo carelessly dared him to his worst.

It was on the fifth day that it happened. Sam was in his office when a servant ran in. 'You're wanted in the house,' the servant panted. 'By Ozigbo.'

When Sam got to the house he saw Ozigbo, his priest-doctor, sitting on the bare ground in the backyard and gnashing his teeth sorrowfully.

'It's Jumbo again!' Ozigbo moaned. 'He wants you to turn into a lunatic.' Immediately he had spoken, he shut his eyes tight and bit his lower lip savagely. He stretched out both hands; spread them wide. His eyes opened. A strange smile showed on his lips. He stood up. Eyes fixed on the ground, he swept the dry brown sand aside with his feet.

'How is it?' Sam inquired anxiously.

'He that seeks to destroy others must be prepared to be destroyed himself,' he murmured. 'Or do you want to spare the fly?'

'No, not at all!'

'The snake that bites stone must lose its fangs,' he said, and picked up his metal staff. 'He that seeks to destroy others must be prepared to be destroyed himself.'

He watched the bare ground silently, with great concentration. Then he took a cool, steady aim. He stabbed. The metallic thud almost shook the ground. 'He's here!' he proclaimed and held the man—whoever it was—there, at the point of the staff, for about a minute.

Not long after, some subdued rumours began to spread. Jumbo had pitched backward, then dropped down, foaming at the mouth ... Sam made no secret about what had happened; he told this story to any who cared to listen. And they were all impressed.

Many things indeed happened in the secret world of charms, Joe reflected. Anyway, such forces had no effect on those who knew nothing about them. He himself knew nothing about charms. In spite of so many convincing manifestations of their reality, he had always refused to have anything to do with charms, whether for protection or for promotion. Once an itinerant trader, a tall, fair and handsome lad, came to him with a leather ball. The ball would protect him from all those that were jealous of his position, so the man said. He took the ball, poured kerosene on it and set it on fire. It burnt to ashes. Anna was present, and she laughed until tears came to her eyes. She laughed even more when the man took to his heels. And the story soon spread throughout Abagwa.

By the time Joe went to bed it was nearly midnight. Even then, he did not sleep until after another thirty minutes. He was thinking about the proposed new building, and he found the thought both pleasant and refreshing.

*

The building was to be started as soon as the first rains had begun to fall. That was what the builders said. Apart from the question of the season—scarcity of water—they had other commitments and could not come earlier. Joe agreed to wait. They were expert builders. He could not find any better.

He had already waited for months. It was now the last week in March and still the rains had not come. The earth was parched, the grass was dead and brown, trees had lost their leaves. He decided he should go to Ania to remind the builders; probably the rain would come any time.

Joe had a late breakfast. He would travel to Obizi on his bicycle, then take a lorry to Ania.

Then Obiakizu ran in. He went straight to the bicycle, held it, and turned the pedal.

'You must carry me on it,' said he with determination.

'No,' Joe replied.

'You must.' He turned the pedal again.

'Is it your own?'

'Please,' he now requested.

Joe lifted him with one hand and sat him on the bicycle frame. He rolled him up and down for a few moments.

'Come down now, you've had enough.'

Obiakuzu sat tight.

'Please come down, I'm travelling a long way.'

Obiakizu still resisted.

He took him down.

'Go back to your father's house. There's nobody to stay here with you.'

'I'll follow you wherever you're going,' replied the boy, clinging to the bicycle. 'I don't want to go to the house.'

'Why?'

'Because Father is not in, and I'm afraid Akueze will beat me. Do you know what happened last night?'

'Tell me.'

'I won't,' he said, then: 'All right, let me tell you. Akueze threw fou fou into Father's face.'

Joe laughed as he had not done for months now.

'I saw it,' he went on. 'I hate Akueze. But is it true Anna will not have children?'

He started. 'Who said so?'

'Akueze. She was telling Mgboli, the one that is Ikeli's wife. That was yesterday, and Father was there.'

'I see,' said he lifelessly. 'And what did your father tell her?'

'Nothing.' He ran off, in pursuit of a big grasshopper which had just flown across.

*

The sun had begun to set on the following day and yet he was not back. That was unusual, Anna thought uneasily. She felt very lonely. Chinwe was away and she was alone in the house. Chinwe had gone to Nade to see her mother who was ill, and would not be back till morning.

Anna sat in the open frontyard, doing nothing, just gazing into the sky where the sun, now a big glowing ball, was sliding steadily down the horizon. All around, birds and insects chirruped as if they were lamenting the impending disappearance of light. There was not a sound of human voice. Not even Obiakizu would call, or cry, or shout this evening. Nor would Akueze, in her usual fashion, call her husband a curse-name.

The clouds were racing furiously. To the direction of Ossa! Anna thought, and a sudden nostalgia gripped her. She remembered about her years of childhood, before Mamma died. In those days they would sit in the frontyard in the evenings gazing at sunset clouds. Then, at night, they would tell folk-stories—she and her brother Andrew.

Andrew was always telling stories about leopards and gorillas. Mamma often appealed to him to change his horrible taste. 'May the leopard eat up your head!' Mamma would sometimes cry in her anger and frustration; and Andrew would shout Amen, smiling. Nobody had heard anything about Andrew for years now. Andrew joined the army even before the war started, without telling her. He told only Brendan, who had been his best friend. Perhaps he was dead already; nobody would be surprised. Andrew had always been a difficult boy. Papa used to say so. Papa shed tears one day because of Andrew.

Her eyes were now nearly wet. But she controlled herself not allowing the tears to spill over. Why should she recall incidents which she had long decided to forget? She would go over to Obieke's house. She would go and tell him that Joe was not yet back. And she would suggest to him that something had gone wrong. Obieke was a pleasant and reasonable man. He would tell her what she should do.

When she was only a few yards from the entrance door to Obieke's compound, she heard loud voices within. She halted and listened. . . . Yes, it was his voice. And Obieke's, too. They were quarrelling.

'I know. That's exactly what I'm saying,' Joe said. 'That land is for my rubber plantation—the whole of it. I intend to clear it as soon as the rains have come.'

'But, Father, we mustn't quarrel because of that,' Obieke pleaded. 'I thought I could cultivate a small portion of it while you took the rest. You see, it has not been cultivated for years now and should give rich tubers.'

'Nobody is quarrelling. You just accept what I've said. That land is for my plantation, and you mustn't touch it.'

'Joe!' her voice dropped—slow, gentle, affectionate. They turned round.

There was silence.

'I heard your voice ringing, from a long distance. Why do you shout at Obieke?'

'Oh, nothing is wrong, wife,' Obieke said. 'We were only talking in loud voices. Father, we had better sort it out later.'

*

'I didn't like the way you were quarrelling with Obieke,' she said to him, just before bed-time. 'Especially after all he has done for us, since our return.'

'It was not a quarrel,' he said lamely, and yawned. 'I only wanted us to get something clearly settled.'

Anna smiled. 'I thought you had stopped settling matters with the fists.'

'Shut up.' Then he began to laugh.

'What is it you want to get settled?'

He deliberated, then said cautiously: 'It's about our family land. We should get it divided, I think, before Akueze—' He had stopped abruptly. She regarded him tensely. 'I'm particularly anxious about Akpaka forest which I told you I would use for my plantation. When I was returning this evening I saw that Obieke had cleared part of it. I've decided I should invite our kinsmen to divide all the family land for us, once and for all. By the way, Mother greets you.'

'You saw her?'

'Yes, on my way back. That was why I came a bit later than usual.'

'How is she?'

'She's well enough. Chinwe will be back tomorrow morning. Mother doesn't want her to return, though.'

'Why?'

'You ought to know. Because you've taken her to the

church. But Chinwe wouldn't listen to that, she'll return.'

Anna was very happy to hear this, for Chinwe had already proved herself quite a girl. She was diligent and down-to-earth in most things, and her sewing was good. One or two Christian mothers had in fact started to make inquiries about her, for their sons.

Fifteen

TWELVE DAYS LATER the kinsmen assembled inside Nwokeji's compound to look into the misunderstanding between Joe and his cousin, Obieke. Everyone of them was there. In the last three days Ikeli, the family elder, had gone round to their respective houses and spoken to them individually. It was a very important matter, he had said. They must put off every other engagement. Never before, at least within living memory, had brother fallen out with brother in Udemezue's family; and it must not be allowed to happen in his own time as the elder, lest the spirits of the dead fathers haunt him for the remaining few hours before his sun would set. They all saw with him; and they promised they would come without fail. And now, they had come in keeping with the promise. Even Willie was present. Willie had travelled all the way from Ania, and was missing an important political lecture on *Divide et Impera*, to be delivered under the auspices of the Youth Liberation Movement of which he was now Publicity Secretary.

As usual, they began with random discussions calculated to wear down ill-feeling before the agenda would come up. Then the conversation centred on the World War.

'I hear the white man known as Itila has iron inside his bones.'

'It's true Jaman is very strong, but Igran has an old man's head.'

'To me they are both the same—brother and brother. Why somebody should fight his brother, I cannot understand.'

'It's madness, nothing else.'

'Left to me, there would be no quarrelling in this world. Not to talk of fighting,' said Uzondu, and several voices answered: 'We know. Not when there's no bone in you!'

Uzondu rummaged in the bag which hung down from his left shoulder, and took out two tablets of aspirin. 'Thank you, Brother,' said he to Joe. 'This medicine you gave me in the morning works wonders. The first two tablets I took apprehended all the evil spirits that were beating drums in my head. They are now making to return—the spirits I mean.' He put the tablets in his mouth.

'Go and swallow them down with water,' Joe advised.

'No, let them dissolve in the mouth, close to the pain. After all, nothing is wrong with my belly.'

Joe tried to persuade him but he had his way.

Nwokeji said: 'Joe, you people who have travelled round the world should know a lot about the war. Why don't you talk while we listen?'

'That's true,' the rest accepted, and they remained silent, waiting for him to speak.

He told them that it was a very big fight—nothing like what they had ever seen, or could imagine. No arrows or knives or spears. Mainly guns. People travelled in the air, inside machines that looked like birds; and under water, inside things that resembled fish. He told them about soldiers who played truant by eating a whole capsule each of alligator pepper. Their mouth temperature would rise as a result; and the white man, concluding that they were sick, would let them off active work or fighting. . . . Before he left Abagwa he heard that the British had a new method of dealing with the Germans. They would hide in small bags below, and from there let holes into German ships and sink them. It was indeed a terrible war, but he thought the British were likely to win.

Fingers snapped in admiration for the British. Many applauded. Thanks to the eloquence of the District Officer at Ossa and his agents and employees, the people of the area were always pleased to hear that the British would win the war.

One person in the gathering felt differently, and that was Willie. And he made no secret of it.

Uppermost in Willie's mind was the liberation of the black race from white rule. Recently he had been elevated from the vague position of Provost to that of Publicity Secretary of the Y.L.M. at Ania, which meant that he was commissioned to spread the gospel of liberation to as wide an area as possible. And he was very well suited for the post. For apart from the fact that he was fearless and stubborn, he was certainly one of the most educated members of the Movement, having read up to Class VI, on Native Authority Scholarship, before he was expelled from a mission secondary school.

That happened with barely six months to the final Cambridge School Leaving Certificate examination. His offence was that he had declared openly, before the principal himself, that a certain prominent nationalist was the Christ of Africa. Not that he didn't believe in God, Willie had gone on to say. For who else but God would have to avenge the wrongs done to the black race? But the principle was not impressed: he ordered Willie to pack his things and leave. The expulsion did not dampen his ardour; rather it had intensified it. And his new post of Publicity Secretary made him all the more zealous now. Such was his enthusiasm at the moment about the thing that he was prepared to hand over, at any time, all his savings, totalling six shillings and nine pence, to anybody, man or monster, white or black, who could crush the imperialists and, automatically, liberate mankind from thraldom.

'It's all wicked propaganda by the British,' he refuted. 'The Germans will win.'

'How do you know?' Joe wondered.

He threatened: 'You wait and see what will happen in the end. The British Empire will just collapse and then we'll rule ourselves.'

They yelled at him. He should rule only himself. Wasn't he mad? It were better everybody ruled in his own compound if it should ever come to self-rule. Speaking seriously, how could they entrust their lives to a few small boys whose only claim to wisdom was that they went to school? But this white man Willie wanted to drive away, was he not the one who brought the lorry which he rode to Ania and back, and the dress he wore? Wouldn't the white man have to take those things back with him if Willie and his type should vex him out of the land? Let Willie find himself a wife first. Let him try to rule just one woman before he could think of extending his authority to the universe!

Willie laughed at their lack of understanding.

'It doesn't interest me much which side wins,' someone now said. 'I like the war in a way, in that some good has come from it. Things sell very well these days. Five years ago palm-oil was like water and palm-kernel was better for fuel than as cash-crop.'

'Very true,' another said. 'A tin of palm-oil gives you as much as four shillings if it's of the transparent, edible type. Everything you touch these days gives you money.'

'You people praise the British, you've not heard that they send our people to India to get killed?' shouted Willie again, over the noises. 'You've not heard?'

They lowered their voices, accepting that there was some

sense in that. He tried to press his advantage:

'They stay out of active fighting and send our own brothers into the field. Then, just think about all the money they're carrying out of our land?'

'They stole that from you, did they?'

He changed tactics: 'They come out as priests and pastors. They ask you to destroy your idol and to do away with our customs. Is that how they did away with their own customs, eh?'

They remarked that he was definitely talking sense this time.

'The Africa Trading Company, Bernards and Sons, J.K.C., and so on—all these companies are here to remove the good things of our land, at a very low price. They pay you as much as four shillings for a tin of palm-oil and you're happy about that! Do you know how much they themselves sell it for?'

'Stuttering!' pronounced Ikeli, a good pinch of snuff on his thumb-nail. 'Would you have been drinking the palm-oil if the white man didn't buy it?'

'And what have you been producing yourself?' another took over. 'I don't like the white man myself for he it was who lit the fire which has been burning the land; but everybody would admit that he brought some good things too.'

'Such as snuff?' Willie replied, and they burst into laughter. Even Ikeli laughed, in spite of the fact that he was blowing his nose at the time.

'But for this scarcity of salt!'

'Fortunately our brother, Joe, has plenty of it,' Uzondu replied. 'Ojukwu of Umudiobia, may you not allow Itila to destroy the world. If it comes to that, I can even go out to fight.'

They began to call him nick-names. Presently, one of them shouted:

'When a man has paid his tax—'

'—then does he have the courage to appear before the white man,' he completed.

'He that maltreats a young palm tree—'

'—rues his offence when time comes for fence-making.'

'When the mouth begins to laugh—'

'—it no longer is able to whistle.'

'The Handwork of an Amateur Taxidermist!'

Silent, he began to prepare his retort.

'When the cock crows for the first time in the morning—' another called.

'—every kind of thief makes haste to escape,' he completed instead.

*

Joe spoke first. He was brief. He would like them to divide Okoli's land between him and Obieke, he said. They should in doing that remember that Okafo, his father, was the elder of the two brothers. Not that he had any immediate need for land, apart from that on which he would grow his rubber plantation, but it was necessary to know which was his own, even if he was not going to use it at once. 'Mine is mine; ours is ours.' That was all, he ended in a rather sharp tone which indicated that something was worrying him.

'You've heard his voice, Obieke, haven't you?' Ikeli asked.

'Yes.' Obieke spoke dully, as if he was indifferent to the whole thing.

'May we now hear your own.'

He was even more brief. He had no quarrel with Joe, he said; and there was nothing wrong. If the kinsmen would fix a day for dividing the family land between the two of them, he would be present. After all he was only a younger son; Joe was the first in the family. 'If I ever think evil of you, Joe, may I'—he pinched the floor—'turn into this sand in my hand!' Then he touched his chest with the clenched fingers.

'Swear not!' they shouted his acquittal. They knew him very well indeed. He would never deliberately offend. They knew how enthusiastic he had been about Joe's return. The two had hitherto blended like salt and oil. Something must have happened. An evil spirit had done it. But they would be equal to the situation.

They sent away the two, and began to discuss. Then they sent away Willie too. The discussion had got to a serious stage. They were now about to express a definite opinion on the matter; and it was necessary that no member of Okoli's family should be present.

They spoke one after the other. First, starting from Nwokeji, the head of each of the five families spoke. Then the more elderly ones. Finally, any who cared to speak.

They were all agreed that there was still goodwill between the two cousins. They also felt that the cause of the disagreement must be traced close to the women—the wives. 'When brothers begin to quarrel over land, trace the cause to the wives.' That was a common saying in the land. It was a statement of fact as well as a proverb. But could Anna be the cause? Probably not; she was a good woman—Anna was, although one could never be certain! Or Akueze? But Obieke wasn't the type that was wife to a woman, or that licked his wife's skin.

Then Ikeli clapped his hands and demanded attention.

'I'm an old man and I see more with my mind than with my eyes,' be began. 'This woman whom Obieke has married for us means to destroy Udemezue's family. She it was who brought about the trouble.'

They interrupted and declared that it was impossible. 'You will please allow his voice to fall,' someone demanded. And when they had subsided Ikeli went on:

'Respect my age and listen to me. I didn't say that Obieke asked her to do anything; or that she asked him to. You see, a bad word poisons the heart.

'I wanted to say it at the start, but I decided I should wait until I had heard you all speak. I'm glad you spoke the way you did. May no evil stay in Udemezue's family—not while I live!' Then he proceeded to invoke the spirits of the dead fathers, starting from Udemezue. The digression heightened the suspense.

'I was saying, she's the cause—Akueze is. Akueze has been mocking our brother and his wife for being childless. She has done so in my hearing more than once, and someone else who heard her came and told me. I believe that must have reached his ears. Naturally, any man who hears such a thing said about him by a woman would think she's speaking the husband's voice. Of course, Akueze couldn't be speaking Obieke's voice; but anger is often blind and does not stop to reason. That's my voice. May everybody live long!'

'And you too!'

Then another spoke, and after him three more.

They drew their seats together, in a small circle, their knees almost touching. Then they spoke in whispers. It was not long before they came to a decision. Joe had nobody yet who would inherit his own share of the land. If he were a bad man—but may Ojukwu of Umudiobia forbid!—he might give away the land to people outside the family. No, the land should remain intact as Okoli's property. When the time came for dividing they would know; there would be no difficulty about that.

'We are agreed on that?'

'Yes!' they chorused.

'But, kinsmen, why don't we ask our brother right away to marry another wife?'

There was a fairly long debate on this. In the end, they decided that the occasion was not proper for such advice. Then they sent for Joe and Obieke; and they appointed two persons—Nwokeji and Ikeli—to be the principal spokesmen.

*

As soon as the cousins were seated, Nwokeji stood up. He raised his right foot and called: 'Ta, nma-nma nu!' and the rest shouted 'Yoh!' in unison. This happened three times.

'May everybody live long!'

'And you, too!' they replied.

Ikeli cleared his throat.

'Okoli, I salute you—I prefer Okoli to that name you call yourself . . . Obieke, I salute you too. . . . The sun has begun to set and those of you who still have limbs—Ikeli isn't one of them!—must go home to tap the palm before it's dark. So, we'll tell you right away what we've decided.'

He searched in his bag. Then he took out a small, black idol.

'Udemezue's family, may nothing evil creep into you!' He touched the idol lightly on the ground, and, simultaneously, they answered: 'Ofo!' But Joe and one other who was a Christian turned away their eyes; and Willie, amused at the reaction, smiled and said something very rude about Christian missionaries.

Ikeli gave a sketch of the family tree. 'So you see,' he concluded, 'we're all the same blood. Stain one finger with oil and the rest will get stained too. If we allow any evil spirit to roost on your own branch of the family, it will extend to the remaining five.

'My sons, this matter between the two of you does not require much deliberation. We came to a decision immediately you left us.' He paused and cleared his throat, for effect. 'Two of you have just been re-united after a separation that started from childhood. It would be most unwise to begin now to divide things between you. No, let the land remain your common possession. Let it be your symbol of brotherhood. But perhaps Nwokeji has something to add.'

'Yes, indeed,' Nwokeji said. 'What you've said so far is very much to our liking.' Then he turned to the two. 'We also wondered what could have brought about such sudden misunderstanding. Whatever it was, we pray that it should go no further than this. All over Umudiobia of ten villages and two, people praise Udemezue's family for its oneness in feeling. We must keep that up. My voice is short. But is it to your liking, my kinsmen?'

'Very much so!' they replied.

'To round up, when the time comes for dividing the land, we'll know. You ought to have no difficulty in agreeing on who should cultivate what portion each year. You have more land then any other in Udemezue's family.'

A few others spoke. They then digressed and began to tell stories, and to call each other names. Everybody laughed and everybody seemed to have forgotten what had brought them together. Then Joe spoke. He thanked them for what they had said; but it appeared from the tone of his voice that he did so with some reservation. And finally, Obieke spoke. He thanked them for the way they had handled the matter.

Sixteen

THE GROUND stretched about a mile from east to west North to south, it rose gently and steadily for about a quarter of a mile. It had last been cultivated two years before and now was being allowed to lie fallow. The vegetation was as yet grass and shrubs interspersed with stunted trees. Lush pasture spread out like deep-green wool in fresh, silent beauty.

You walked across this slope. Then you came to a big forest. The forest separated Umudiobia and Ozala. At the thick eastern end it was about a mile deep, and tapered at the west where a foot-path linked the two towns. Its total area was about ten acres, perhaps more. It was well known not only in Umudiobia but also to all the towns around. It was much dreaded, too.

This was Akpaka forest.

Akpaka had, in the distant past, been a public dumping place for the abominable, such as twin babies or ones deformed. It used to be, also, the graveyard for those who died a bad death, by which was meanth death from white disease, smallpox, hernia, and bloated belly, or any of those sicknesses which disfigured the victim's face and robbed his body of the form of man. Such bodies must not be consigned to earth in the same way as those of the clean. Akpaka also received the bodies of those that died evil deaths—murderers, robbers, perjurers—all those who committed some outrageous offence against custom or religion. Such people were either put to death outright and their bodies thrown into the forest; or they were left there to expire slowly as a penalty for their offence. Their bodies must lie unburied and provide rich nourishment for things that flew in the air and things that crept on the surface of the earth; their spirits must be left to wander about in agony, for endless ages, since they received no burial or funeral obsequies; they would never be reincarnated in this world.

All that was before Udemezue cleared the forest, about sixty years back. Legend had it that Udemezue was the very first man since creation to touch Akpaka with a matchet; and that the spirits which had dwelt inside it had, before then, a special way of scorching some of the vegetation dead.

What led Udemezue to do it was still a matter for speculation. Some, mostly his many descendants, said he wanted to make his name immortal by daring what nobody else had done. He was only thirty years old then, and he was tall and stout. As a warrior, he took more heads than any of his age in Umudiobia and around. And he was a famous hunter, and a champion wrestler in his younger days. Having proved himself great in the things of mortals, Udemezue thought of doing something which the immortals alone had been able to do. And what came readily to his mind was to clear Akpaka forest. Many however held that the act was only in accord with his greedy nature; that he merely wanted the land. He was daring, it was true; but he was ruthless and cruel in the extreme. He used his gift of strength to oppress and he deprived people of their land, wives or daughters. Indeed, several shocking stories were still current about the tyranny, savagery and avarice of the legendary hero who in his tantrums stamped his feet heavily and the ground vibrated.

Whatever must have been his real motive, Udemezue did not find the task an easy one. The first thing he did was to retain a team of priest-doctors in his house to fortify his body and spirit. And the priest-doctors worked for one moon on end. During this time he talked to nobody; he did not leave his compound; he ate but one meal each day; and he would not taste anything that a woman's hand had touched. Then, one morning, he set out to attack the forest.

He had a bundle of matchets, all double-edged. He was stark naked—apart from the charms round his neck, his waist, and his thighs and forearms. He was chewing something in his mouth. It was said that the whole of Iboland felt the shock on that first day his matchet touched the woods, and people hurriedly offered sacrifices to the gods, and every seer made brisk business. Anyway, Udemezue went on, resting only a few hours before and after midnight, while his team of priest-doctors intensified their efforts, strengthening his mind, heart and will, as well as his body.

The forest ceased to exist after six moons. Then Udemezue set on fire those trees which his matchet could not fell. The flames ate into the bones and marrow, up to the limbs and down to the roots, of the tall trees which for ages had defied everything—rain, sun, and wind. As the explosions resounded, Udemezue boasted from his obi that it was his name that was ringing throughout Iboland; but others remarked that the gods were groaning from the depths of the earth. People foretold very terrible things for the land.

Indeed their fears did come true. First, Udemezue himself died. He died only a year after, at an unripe age of thirty years and two, less some months. He started by making some hissing sounds; then he began to shake spasmodically; finally, blood gushed out of his mouth and he dropped down dead. A few minutes later, his body began to decompose.

Then, two years after, the first batch of white men landed at Ania and, from there, carried into the hinterland the fire that was now consuming the entire area. That came as a result of the disappearance of Akpaka forest! Some of the spirits that had escaped had now come back to the land in the form of white men. For whoever saw human beings with that type of skin, who gibbered like monkeys when they were supposed to be talking, and who had no toes at all? Some had gone into men's hearts: no wonder human beings were now so susceptible to evil. And many others had come down from the world of spirits, out of sheer sympathy, and were now creating confusion among men.

Udemezue's first son, and Nwokeji's grandfather, had refused to touch the land where Akpaka forest had stood. It was Okoli, the second son, who inherited it—that was why his grandsons had much more land than any other branch of the extended family. Okoli cultivated the land only once during his life time.

Amanze was a coward. Everybody knew that. He cultivated only a small strip, on the border. It was reported that he held his heart in his hand each time he approached the place. Anyway, nothing seemed to have happened to him as a result, for he lived up to the comparatively ripe age of fifty-five. And although on his death-bed he told his first son, Obieke, that the spirits had abandoned the place completely, Obieke was still afraid. Obieke cultivated the ground only once, which was six years back. Even then, he cultivated only a small part himself; the rest he leased out to the Christians who didn't seem to care (anything) about spirits, good or evil.

This then was the place Joe selected for his rubber plantation. Ever since he returned to Umudiobia, he had been studying the spot with his keen professional eye. Deep-green, voluptuous, foliage. And it was extensive. It would be ideal.

*

Ikeli had not been completely satisfied with the action taken at the meeting of the kinsmen. He felt that something more must be done to bring the two cousins together, as before. But he kept this to himself. A thing like that must not be shouted out in public; it required tactful, unobtrusive action. He would visit Obieke one day—and that soon—and speak to him.

He did so on the fourth day. He told Obieke how Akueze had brought about the disagreement between him and Joe. Akueze had wounded Joe's heart. It was necessary that he should do something about it. Then Obieke stormed, and threatened he would beat up his wife. But Ikeli merely laughed and wondered when it was he turned into a fool. Beat a woman? No, he should just set his mind on reassuring his brother.

From that day, Obieke visited Joe's house at least once each day. Sometimes he went with a jar of wine, which they drank together, conversing. At times he would send for Anna to his house and give her some yams to cook for her husband; he would also bid her to take good care of her husband.

And then, the time came for clearing the forest. Obieke offered to give up the portion he had already cleared for his farm. Joe objected, but Obieke insisted. He was not giving up the land in anger, Obieke said, and affirmed with an oath. Let Joe have it since he wanted a large area for his plantation. At that, Joe smiled, pleasantly, and swore he would not touch the portion. He would also leave off the part of the forest that adjoined that portion. . . . And that was how the issue came to be finally resolved. Unconsciously, the two had portioned the land between them. Obieke had about a quarter of the total area while Joe took the rest.

Men of Umudiobia were still afraid to enter Akpaka; and besides, they were not particularly industrious. Especially at this season when the palm poured its wine like rain water and there were yams to eat! So Joe was compelled to go outside the town to hire labour.

As a matter of fact, he did not go in person: again, it was Obieke that went. Obieke went to Ogolo, which was nearly ten miles away. And many people gladly offered to come from there, for they were promised they would be paid some money for the work—as much as one penny if they worked from morning till evening. But no breadfruit!

For a penny each day, the labourers came, all the way, and the work that would have taken Umudiobia several weeks to complete was over in just ten days, and for the sum of fifteen shillings.

*

The builders had arrived at long last. They went round and inspected the site. Then they listed three things which must be done before they could even touch the ground with their shovels. First, he must assure than that there would be steady supply of both cement and palm-wine. Second, they would warm up their bodies with a goat, hoof to horn. Third, there would be a foundation-laying ceremony. A brief argument followed. Joe got them to commute the goat to two big cocks. Then they fixed a day for the foundation-laying.

Oral invitations went out. All well-wishers were invited, in general. Special message went to the Catholic church committee of which Jerome was still the head, and to the teachers, and to the umuada. Willie got the Freedom Crusader, a daily newspaper at Ania, to announce: 'The construction of the domiciliary edifice of Mazin Nnanna Okafo, retired Forest Guard, of Abagwa fame, will be initiated at Umudiobia on the 10th April 1943 with a grand ceremony. Eminent personalities will grace the occasion, and the chairman will be Mazi B. Akosa Higher Elementary, plus London Matriculation (Attempted).'

For the umuada the occasion presented the first real opportunity to let the world know what they felt about their brother. They refused to attend—all of them without a single exception. 'What is the need building a house for rats and lizards?' they asked, and sighed in anger. On the other hand, quite noticeably, a good number of people came who were members of the Anglican Church. They were mostly the younger ones, aged anything between eighteen and thirty-five. This was in spite of the fact that the committee of the Anglican Church at Umudiobia had prescribed a fine of six pence on any of their members who would be present at the function, and had appointed two persons to watch out for defaulters.

The chairman (who incidentally was not Akosa) opened with a longish prayer. He prayed that Almighty God would speed up the work when once started. He prayed that the builders would finish the work without a single scratch on their bodies. Then he wished Joe and Anna a very long life, so that 'you'll do the house'. So far he had spoken in Ibo, but he completed his prayer in English—'enjoy.'

Drinks were served. At the same time, others spoke. One thanked God for sparing Joe's life and bringing him back to his people. Another showered praises on Anna for feeding the husband well and thereby giving him the peace of mind that must have led to such ideas. Another made sly remarks about the Anglicans, 'the hidden snakes', and challenged them to produce such a great figure. The fourth speaker was an Anglican. He welcomed the builders into the land and assured them of the people's hospitality. He had not quite listened to what the last speaker had said, he added; but he had an idea the man was being narrow-minded. The fifth appealed to the natives to send their children to church and school. He received a big boo in reply.

Two persons stood up simultaneously. One was Willie; the other was Jerome. Willie sat down again, in deference to the other's age. But he would not remain quiet. He began to preach liberation. Willie said rude things about white men, and his fellow black men who sat round him gave equally rude retorts. There was considerable noise and confusion. Jerome surveyed the entire gathering, wide-eyed, and two elderly volunteers rose and began to shout 'That's enough, everybody!'

'In the name of the Father—' Jerome intoned.

'—and of the Son and of the Holy Ghost, Amen,' they responded.

His theme was the impossibility of serving God and Mammon. He started in a slow, condescending tone. Then his voice developed, and he spoke with feeling. The crowd listened with concentration. Indeed he was a good orator and, in spite of his sixty years, he still had a strong personality: he was tall, though with a slight stoop; and he had been a very handsome man in his younger days. He wore a silk shirt, white and neat, over a georgette wrapper, which was a symbol of status among the people.

A surprising thing happened when he ended. Some clapped, but many booed and their voices drowned the clapping. A few muttered something about the church being nobody's personal property.

*

'It was very grand, I thought,' Anna said. That was later that day, in the night. 'But for that man!'

'Who?' asked Joe.

'Jerome. You shouldn't have invited him.'

He laughed. 'Leave him. It's good, in a way, that he came. Didn't you see what happened in the end?'

'The boo?'

'Yes.'

'Why did they do that?'

'I think I know. You could notice it was the younger members of the church who booed. They don't like his ways. They say he behaves as if he owns the place, as if others are there by sufferance. They are now beginning to rebel.'

'He deserves it then. Each time he comes here he talks about riches. As if you stole his money!'

'He's jealous. He feels I'm a danger to his authority among the church members.'

'Only may that not affect the church in a bad way,' Anna said.

Seventeen

THE HOUSE THAT was being built became the talk of the town. Many came to see how the expert masons were setting stone blocks in cement mortar. And the latter, flattered by the visits, whistled some catchy tunes and manipulated their trowels with extra grace. One told stories of how he had nearly been employed in the Public Works Department at Ania. Another claimed that it was he who built the District Officer's garage at Ossa. The stories impressed the visitors. The rumour spread that the men were the best masons in the world; and that they had played an important part in the building of the big church at Ania.

Then, on the twentieth day of the start of the work, Chiaku came. The time was noon. Anna and Chinwe were in the house. Anna had returned only the day before, after a week's visit to Ania; and she did not go to the workshop today.

'He-i, Mother!' Chinwe cried out. 'I thought you said you would never come here again.'

She frowned and winked; then she turned away her face.

'So you've changed your mind at last, after so many months?' She gave a teasing smile.

'Yes, I have,' Chiaku snapped. 'And that amuses you, does it?'

She laughed.

'Bad, stubborn child! But I'm not surprised: you're like

him, that's why you choose to remain here. You joined the church in spite of all I've said.' She sat down.

'Can I come and take you to the church next Sunday?'

She stood up again, suddenly. 'May your mouth be sealed, evil one!' she cursed in her anger, and then turned to Anna. 'Please take me to the place where you people are building the new house.'

Soon they came to the site. She snapped her fingers and shrugged, and exclaimed, in admiration. But, a few minutes later, she demanded:

'Please let's go back.'

'What's wrong?' Anna asked.

Silent, she began to move away. Anna followed her. The masons looked on in surprise.

They were now out of earshot. Chiaku halted, turned round and sobbed. Anna too halted.

'So you're still like that?' Pause. 'That a man should undertake to build such a house for rats and lizards, and snakes!'

Anna withered.

'I thought you told me you were taking some treatment. So it has had no effect?' Her voice rose. 'But I knew it would be like this. Why then do I now ask? I knew it from the day he joined the church. . . . Okafo my husband, so that's what your chi had intended for you? Tfia!' she spat hard and venomously, into the air before her, at the evil spirit which had been working in her son.

Anna related all this to Joe after supper, before bed, last night.

She was now twenty-five years old—if the truth must be told; and she was still beautiful in look and elegant in build. But the skin of her face had begun to slacken, prematurely. People said this was the effect of the concoctions she had been drinking into her stomach, but in actual fact what worried her more than anything else was the attitude of the women who were Joe's relatives, especially the things they now said publicly, sometimes in her hearing.

'Your husband is building a wonderful house,' someone would compliment.

'You've not mentioned that he's refused to be a father,' they would sing—as many as four voices at the same time. Then one of them would add: 'But does it bother him? It doesn't.'

'That's true, Sister,' another would say, 'He's even growing fat.'

'I wonder why our brothers can't talk to him openly about that.'

'They may have tried. But do you think he will ever listen to anybody's advice when it comes to that?'

'If that is what going to church means I would rather cut off my son's head with a blunt knife than allow him to join them. . . .'

Sometimes it happened that some church women were present. In that case, the conversation would run like this:

'But he has become rich by joining the church, hasn't he? You can't see that side of it?'

'Rich? What's the use of riches when there's nobody—one's own blood—to inherit them? When they cannot secure the obi?'

'Maybe God will answer our prayer on Anna's behalf one of these days.'

'Maybe when the earth has met the sky!'

'I don't like your tongue. . . .'

One day Adagu went to the extent of swearing never to talk to either Joe or Anna again in her life.

That happened in the market. Anna was not there; it was a friend who later brought the story to her. 'Let him die and be forgotten rather than continue to cause us so much distress,' Adagu had said in a broken, distressed voice. People hushed her. Then her heart melted and her eyes brimmed over. It was said Adagu wept that day until the market was beginning to disperse; she then swore never in her life to talk to Joe or Anna again. And yet, it was only a passing remark, thrown into the wind, that had started it all. Somebody, a fellow woman, had said that with as many as ten grand-sons in her father's family, the obi was solid and intact. The woman was merely rejoicing at news, just received, that her brother's wife was delivered of a male child. Adagu overheard her and thought it was a wicked remark intended for her.

A few days after the incident, Adagu and Anna met face to face, for the first time in several weeks. That was in Obieke's house. Anna greeted Adagu who replied distantly; in fact, she merely grunted.

'You've not been visiting us again.'

'You know why, don't you?' she replied sharply, forgetting her oath.

'Do I?'

'Tell me, please, have you made some medicine to hold our brother to yourself alone?'

'How?'

'So that he doesn't think about any other thing apart from yourself: he doesn't even think of his father's obi.'

'Shut up, Adagu!' Obieke shouted and looked up at her from the climbing rope which he was re-padding at the moment.

'Look, we'll have no objection if you bring your own sisters for him to marry, provided they bear for us.'

'Didn't I say shut up?'

She held her tongue. She always obeyed and respected him. It started from their childhood days when they used to play together in a sandy shade. He used to be her husband, and she used to obey all his commands.

*

'They are very wicked, all those women who call themselves your sisters,' Anna complained in an exasperated tone.

Joe said nothing. The usual vein stood out on his forehead, seeming to pulsate. His eyes half-closed, Joe gazed with concentration at the crucifix that hung on the wall directly opposite him. It seemed as if that crucifix had more meaning for him this night than ever before. He was sitting turned away from Anna, who could not see the expression on his face.

'I've never seen such wicked people in my life, honestly. They taunt one with one's ill luck.'

He was still silent.

'Very, very, very wicked!'

'Why don't you tell them something in reply?' he asked now without much life or interest.

'Like what?'

'Anything.'

'I've nothing to tell them. God will do that for me one day.'

'Then it's your fault.'

'My fault?'

'Yes, you should have found something equally painful to tell them. But stop bothering my ears.' He turned, facing her directly.

'I see,' Anna retorted. 'I should find something to tell them! You seem to forget that I'm a stranger in Umudiobia. They are your sisters; it's you who should speak to them.'

He relapsed into silence. His legs began to shake.

'I think it's better that you go and marry as they have been advising you to do. Don't let anybody say again that Anna is in your way.'

He regarded her fiercely.

'I know that's what you've been telling them all the time.'

'Will you shut up now!'

She clicked her tongue defiantly.

'Your mouth stinks!'

'Yes, let it stink, but go and marry. Go this night, please.'

He sprang up from his seat. 'Say it again!' he bawled out and stepped towards her. 'Go on, say it again!'

She could see in the light of the lamp burning on the table behind her that his eyes were red and his whole body was shaking. Fear seized her; she began to pant. She had remembered he was like that the day he beat Jerry Eziem until Jerry collapsed on the ground.

'Go on, talk now!'

Tears filled her eyes.

She went out to the frontyard to hide herself in the thick darkness. He flared into abuse. He called her a fool, and idiot, a villain, a devil and other names. But she shut her mouth tight and held her breath. It would soon end and he would forgive and forget, but while it lasted it must receive no fuel. Joe's anger burnt like the fire which consumed dry reed. All you needed to do was to isolate it and let it burn out; then, within a short time, you could have your husband back. . . . He would soon recover from it. She understood him just too well. Throughout their seven years of marriage, they had not had any serious quarrel, and he had never attempted to strike her with his hand or with a stick.

That was because she knew him like the palm of her hand: She knew by instinct the right moment to retreat, the right moment to come back to him, and the right attitude and language which would compel his forgiveness. And when she had her own fits of temper, he would remain quiet or merely regard her with an indulgent smile. Except this night. . .

About thirty minutes later, Anna began to return to the house. She moved in slow penitent steps. Then when she had got to the edge of the corridor she gave a dry cough.

He peeped out. 'You had better come in.'

She did so hesitantly.

Not one word was spoken between them again that night. Each went to bed almost immediately.

She woke before him in the morning. She rose noiselessly and walked into his room. She observed his face. He was still asleep. She shook him, gently, until he was awake.

He wiped his face mechanically with the palm of his right hand.

'Is it daybreak already?'

'Almost.'

He lay still and silent again.

She knelt down besides the bed. She pushed him gently, as before.

'What?'

She clasped her hands as if she was about to pray. She said to him: 'Joe, please forgive me. It was the work of the devil.'

'What was?'

'I mean about last night.'

Silence again.

'Have you now forgiven me?'

He smiled.

*

In the night of the following day, after supper, he asked her:

'What about the medicine Emenike gave you?'

Anna hesitated. 'I had wanted to tell you about it. It's extremely bitter, and not only that, it has been beating a drum inside my stomach for weeks now.'

'Why not stop taking it? I've noticed a change in the colour of your skin. You now look like an etiolated fruit.'

'Obieke said the same thing today. Let's not pay any more money to Emenike.'

'But we've already paid the full amount. He kept on demanding some amount each time he met either myself or Obieke.'

'Of course they always behave like that. . . . Is there any other doctor I could try?'

'I don't know of any. But, hadn't you better give your body another rest?'

Anna heaved. 'Or could it be that the failure was due to absence of that thing?'

'What?'

'The thing he said I should wear?'

'The leather belt, is it?'

'Yes.' Her voice was barely audible.

He tried to think, and he pulled his lips back.

'Do you want to try it?'

'I don't know,' Anna said. 'We might. Or shouldn't we?'

'I'll ask Obieke,' he said after a pause.

Eighteen

FOR THE NEXT few days she was utterly restless. She moved clumsily and nervously. At times she would halt, turn and look round, like one haunted by invisible shapes.

On the night of the fifth day she lay wide awake and thrashed about until the early hours of morning. Her conscience was tormenting her. 'You're trying to deceive God, are you?. . . . She's no excuse, the headmaster's wife isn't. . . . The catechism is definite about it: "The First Commandment forbids divination, pagan sacrifices, charms. . . . " That belt is a charm.' It was with such words that the silent voice pricked Anna's mind for hours on end that night.

She woke up well after the sun had risen. Joe had left for the rubber plantation and Chinwe was sweeping the yard. She knelt down beside the bed, a chaplet in her hand, and began to pray. But the words stopped short of her heart and her hand trembled and her head swelled with fear.

Some five minutes passed.

Anna put the chaplet back under her pillow. She stood up and began to undress. Soon she pulled the belt down her waist, down her legs, until it had dropped on the ground. She left it there and began to dress again.

Then she picked up a packet of matches from the table. She took a bottle of kerosene from under the table. She picked up the leather belt. She tied these together with a scarf.

She went out. As yet she had no definite destination. But when she had gone some hundred yards from the house she entered the bush on the left. There, in an open space, she untied the scarf, dropped the belt on the ground. She poured some kerosene on it. Then she struck a match.

Anna watched the leather belt as it burnt. And, as if to re-affirm her decision, she poured more and more kerosene, so much that she nearly emptied the bottle and the flame continued to burn even after the leather had been reduced to ashes. She crushed the ashes. With that, she felt a sense of release and a return of inward peace. She would pray to God for forgiveness. She would pray to the Holy Mother for intercession. And she would pray to her patron saint too.

*

She was preparing to leave for her workshop the following day when the headmaster's wife entered.

'I went to see some of our church women in this part of Umudiobia,' the latter said. 'I thought I should drop in to see you. Anything wrong?'

'No. Why?' Anna replied rather coldly.

'Because you look sad.'

'I'm not.' She gave a cheerless smile. 'Did you know I tried that thing afterwards?'

'What thing?'

'The leather belt.'

'Oh, very good. You wait and see the result.'

She nodded cynically. 'I've burnt the nonsense.'

'You did what?' Asked the other with a start.

'I decided to.'

'But you can't be serious.'

'I burnt it yesterday,' Anna said, then changed the topic.

'I wonder if you could come and help me one evening,' she asked.

Anna began by objecting, then asked what it was about.

'To cut the pattern for a new dress I want to sew,' she said. 'You know I'm not conversant with the new patterns—at least not as much as you.'

They left the house together, and on their way they fixed both the day and the time.

*

Anna said to her: 'I hope you were not upset at the way I treated you when you came to our house.'

'How?' She asked.

'I was a bit distant.'

'Oh, not at all! We're friends after all and friends should be prepared to disagree from time to time.'

'I think I must hurry back now.'

She had been there, in the headmaster's house, for hours now, cutting the patterns. Twilight had set in. She rose and beat off the scraps of cloth on her dress.

'I'll see you off,' the other offered.

They were about fifty yards away from the house, near the fence which bordered the school compound. The headmaster's wife halted and Anna halted too, from sheer infection.

'Anna, now that you've burnt that leather belt what else are you going to do?'

'You still think about that thing?' Anna replied. 'But why do you ask?'

'N-nothing. But, I was just wondering, are you sure it's your fault? Don't you think it could be his?'

'Whose?'

'Your husband's. Although men would always blame the women.'

Anna just grimaced.

The last trace of light was now about to disappear. Two of them stood face to face, like conspirators planning the night's adventure.

'It's possible you've been suffering because he's deficient.'

At this point, a shape appeared in the still imperfect darkness. Anna was the first to see it and she drew the other's attention to the direction. They watched the figure advance, towards them, in slow, measured steps, hands inside the pockets.

'Oh, it's Mr Ejim,' the headmaster's wife said. 'He's the Agricultural Superintendent at Eziko. The man speaks good of you.'

'Of me? How did he get to know me?' Anna asked, quite embarrassed.

'He must have been seeing you in your workshop. Do you know, his wife has had seven children of whom only one is a girl.'

'He's very lucky,' Anna replied naively.

She grinned. 'May be you would like to try him?'

'What did you say?' She was still trying to obtain an answer to her question when the man, Mr Ejim, arrived. He stood before them, hands in the pockets and feet astride. 'Who are these?' said he, expansively. 'Oh, I see, it's the headmaster's michich.'

'Good evening, sir!'

'Good evening. And who's the other? Doesn't she greet?'

'Sir, she is my good friend.'

'I think I've seen her somewhere before.' Then he looked very close—indeed dangerously close—into Anna's face. Anna stepped backwards and glared venmously, first at the headmaster's wife, then at the Agricultural Superintendent.

'Perhaps, sir, we can see her off together. It's dark already.'

'Sure, sure,' the official accepted. 'I can even do that alone. Good lady,' said he in English, 'I'm Mr Ejim. I inspect all the school farms in this District.' He advanced and stretched out his hand to hold her wrist. She resisted. Then he moved closer still, until he had brought his handsome face to within a few inches of her lips.

Anna replied with both her mouth and her finger-nails. She did wonders with her tongue, and even greater wonders with her fingers, on the man's face that evening.

*

She must not tell him about it, resolved she within herself. In her younger days she would have done so. But she had learnt her lesson—since that day he nearly beat Jerry Eziem to death. She would never tell him again lest he should kill somebody one day. And so, Anna had kept to herself all that evil men had been telling her. But, just as in the present case, she did not let such men go scot free. She would face them direct with her tongue and saliva, and, if need be, with her finger-nails too. She was after all a strong woman and could look after herself. No, she must not tell him; she would tell Obieke instead.

She did so the next morning.

'Good wife,' Obieke commended. 'I've always said you were well brought up. Tell me, does he know about it?'

'Joe?'

'Yes.'

'No; I haven't told him.'

'Please don't. And tell nobody else. You must also keep away, in future, from both the teacher and his wife.' He shrugged with his left shoulder. 'Church men!' sneered he and shrugged once more. 'I thought that man was Father's good friend. And now he wants to give his friend's wife to another man.'

'But it was not he; it was the wife that played the devil.'

He shook his head. 'You are a woman. I've seen the whole thing as any sensible man would. Anway, do as I've told you.' He paused. 'I owe you something for your great virtue. I'll bring a hen over to you in the evening.'

Joe was in when he brought the hen.

'For some very commendable act,' he said as he handed it over to her. 'Father, we won't let you know what it is.'

'Thank you,' Anna replied, smiling. 'No, we won't tell him.'

'This wife you've married into our family is very good indeed, my brother.'

When Obieke left, Joe tried to find out what it was that had won her the prize of a young hen which had just begun to lay. But Anna refused to disclose. 'You heard what he said, didn't you?' said she in jest. 'We won't tell you.' Then she called Chinwe and handed over the hen to her. She told her to tether it to a big stick and give it some feed.

'Joe!' She called after some time, studying his face with the corner of her eyes.

'What?'

'Why in that tone?'

'I wasn't angry.'

'Only moody, perhaps. What has upset you this morning.'

'N-nothing' said he and asked: 'Do you still wear that belt?'

'Why do you ask?' asked she with a smile.

'You better throw it away.'

'Are you serious?'

'Yes. Throw it away. It's sin. We shouldn't have touched it at all.'

'Maybe that's what has been worrying your mind.'

'Go and throw it away,' he repeated in the tone of a command.

Anna drew her seat closer, towards him. 'I should have told you, but I was afraid you would be angry with me. I destroyed it seven days ago.

He came suddenly to life. 'You did?'

'I burnt it myself. And I crushed the ashes with my feet.'

'I'm happy you did. I don't know what devil drove us into it.'

'I know. It's the headmaster and his long-beaked wife,' Anna replied. 'But God will set the two of them ablaze one day, in the same way I burnt the belt!' There was much bitterness in her voice.

He laughed.

Nineteen

AT ABOUT eight o'clock that morning six apprentices seamstresses came and removed the sewing machine and materials to the workshop. Shortly after, Chinwe too left. Only Joe and Anna were now in the house. In ordinary circumstances, they would both now leave for work.

They went on talking, desultorily. They moved from Uzondu to the War; then they discussed the rubber plantation, trade in salt and the new building. Joe did most of the talking and Anna added a few words now and then, smiling. She was very happy this morning. It was the first time, for several days now, Joe had talked freely like this. Indeed she had been very much worried about his reticence, more still by his tendency to move dreamily and allow things to drift. He seemed to have shrunk completely within himself.

The time was now nearly half-past nine.

'Let me go in and prepare for work,' Anna said, and she rose. She went into her room.

'I too should be leaving for the rubber plantation,' Joe said.

A few minutes passed. 'Are you there?' she asked again; then again.

She tiptoed out, into the sitting-room, then into the kitchen.

He was already raising a sizeable piece of dried fish into his mouth. 'Ey-i-i!' she exclaimed; and she slapped him hard on the elbow. 'Daylight rogue!' she protested. In reply Joe broke the fish into two and offered her one part, which she accepted. But she did not eat it; she put it back in the basket. Then she began to leave.

She wore wrapper and blouse, of the same fabric. It was brown check on a pinkish foundation, and it blended exquisitely with the copper-colour of her skin. She moved with an unconscious grace. Each step brought the full weight of her body squarely and solidly on the ground.

'You seem to be celebrating today,' he remarked from the edge of the corridor.

Anna turned. 'Don't you think we should?'

'Perhaps you're right. You look very beautiful anyway.'

'You've just discovered that you have a very beautiful wife, have you?'

They laughed together. Anna continued to laugh until she was some distance from the house.

He would have left for the plantation almost immediately, but he had two sets of visitors. The first was Uzondu, and he came for nothing in particular. Joe managed to dismiss him with a free gift of half a cup of salt. After that, he picked up his matchet and took out his bicycle. It was then that Obiakizu and his half-sister came in.

Obiakizu was running, dragging the little girl by the hand. Their bodies were stained with wood ash and there were charcoal marks on their faces as they had been roasting some palm-nuts in their father's obi.

'Where are you going now?' Obiakizu asked.

'To Akpaka. You both look like pigs. What have you been doing?. . . . Tah, don't touch me.' He stepped aside.

They looked from his brown helmet to the brown shirt,

down to the brown shorts and brown canvas shoes. 'I like your dress,' Obiakizu said; 'but don't go away, we've come to visit you.'

'Not now, I'm going out to work,' he replied gently.

Obiakizu held the bicycle frame with his left hand and rotated the pedal with the right. 'Touch it, Ijeoma,' he said. But the girl stepped backward in fear. 'Come on, it won't bite you,' he laughed.

'I've told you, Obiakizu, never to touch that pedal again, haven't I,' Joe said. 'Or don't you hear with those big ears of yours?'

'I do,' he replied seriously and invited his half-sister, once more, to help herself. Still, Ijeoma refused. Then he rotated the pedal again.

'I'll beat you if you don't remove your hand,' Joe objected, and bending down, he slapped the hand on the pedal. As he did so he noticed that the rear tyre was flat. He sighed. Then he leaned the bicycle against the wall, and locked it.

'You're not taking it with you?' Ijeoma wondered.

'No.'

'Why?'

'It's spoilt.'

'Then give it to us,' Obiakizu suggested and fixed his eyes longingly on the bicycle. 'Go and buy another one for yourself.'

'I see.' He took it inside.

'Go back now, I'm going to the rubber plantation,' said he.

'We'll follow you. Ijeomea, come along,' Obiakizu replied.

'To Akpaka?'

'Yes.' He dragged the girl by the hand.

'It's a long distance from here, and you won't be able to get there.'

'We will.'

Ijeoma added: 'We'll run.'

Indeed they ran, after him. He hastened his steps. They ran faster.

'What will you be doing when you get there?' Obiakizu asked.

'I'll work.'

'You'll dig yams?'

'No. There are no yams there.'

Ijeoma cried: 'See, see, see that grasshopper there! On the cassava twig!'

They watched the insect for some moments.

'I'll catch it for you if you will go back after that,' Joe offered.

'Agreed,' Obiakizu replied. But Ijeoma hushed them both and instructed them to speak only in whispers.

He stepped slowly, gently, into the bush, sweeping the foliage out of his way with his hands.

'Go noiselessly, please,' Ijeoma advised expertly, still in a whisper. 'When you get near enough you stretch out your hand and catch it for us. Remember to clench your fingers when you've caught it.'

He had come within two feet of the cassava plant. He reached out his hand. But the green insect spread out its wings, spitefully, and flew away, far into the bush.

They continued to follow him when he had come out from the bush. They even ran past him. 'Yoh!' they jeered. 'You can't even catch a small grasshopper.' He laughed.

'Obiakizu, see that bird flying up in the sky,' Ijeoma said a few minutes later. They both halted. 'Let him catch it for us.'

'He can't.'

'Why?'

'Don't you see it flies high up in the sky.'

'Then let him throw a club at it. Good, it has perched. See it on that small tree.'

'That's probably its home. It lives there with its mother and brothers and sisters.'

'Do they go to church?'

'Look, he's gone far. Run!'

They ran until they had caught up with Joe. They even overtook him and kept a regular distance in front. But soon, his saviour appeared.

'Ye-e-ei!' they exclaimed together.

'What again?'

'It's ochukwudo!' Their eyes focused on the two lazy, rotund grasshoppers, spotted red and green, which had perched on the twigs. Before he would say a word, the children fell on the insects. He took the opportunity to escape.

*

The seeds had been planted several weeks before. The shoots had now bored through, to the surface of the earth, as would a late moon through the sky. There were hundreds, thousands, of them. Joe went from one end of the plantation to the other and examined the shoots. Some were already a few inches high. They were all yellow, tender and delicate; and they looked as pure and innocent as puppies just come to life. It gave him a deep, almost spiritual, pleasure. As a Forest Guard he had enjoyed tending rubber plants both at Abagwa and in towns around. And now he was growing his own plantation—a promising one indeed, on a rich soil and in suitable climate. So Joe reflected as he removed the shrubs and creepers which grew dangerously close to the shoots. Some he uprooted with his hands, the others he cut carefully with the matchet.

Then his mind went to the future. In a few years' time the plants would have grown up, ready for tapping. He would hire some labourers for that. He knew the method himself; he would teach the labourers. They would make scars in the barks of the trees, and would tie small containers underneath the scars. Into the containers would drip the milk-white bleed. This bleed was the rubber itself—rubber which was in so great a demand. Many indeed had become rich in other lands, because of rubber, because of the war. This was the fifth year of the war. Nobody knew when it would end. Just two weeks before, the District Officer had sent one more important notice which was read out in the church. 'If you can't join the army,' the notice had said, 'then you must produce palm-oil or kernel, or rubber. These things will help to win the war against the enemy of mankind. And even if the war should now end, the commodities would still be in great demand.'

Suddenly, he felt a sharp, sucking pain down in his ankle. He bent down, slowly; then he hit, bringing down his whole weight vengefully on the savage tse-tse fly. Then, as he was trying to wipe the blood stains on the sole of his shoes somebody called.

'Did you hear?' Willie asked.

'What?'

'About the war.'

'No. Have your friends, the Germans, won?'

'They are not my friends,' Willie corrected. 'But the British imperialists are certainly my enemies, for they hold mankind in thraldom. Anyway, the news is that the war in North Africa is over.'

'True?'

'Yes. The Germans have been beaten.'

'Thank God!'

'Although the main war continues. Let them clear out of our continent,' he said, and pointed proprietorily to the ground. 'Let them go home and fight there.' Then he continued to talk about liberation. But Joe was no longer listening; he was humming a tune instead.

'I forgot to tell you, Joe,' said Willie after some time.

'What? I hope it's nothing to do with liberation.'

'Anna asked me to inform you she's going to Ozala straight from her workshop. She says she's going to Confession or something like that.'

'Oh, I see. So Father is going to Ozala today?'

'So I hear. But tell me, Joe my brother, why do you people allow yourself to be fooled with an imported religion?'

'Stop your nonsense!' he objected. 'I'm going away now—and to Confession too, if you care to know.'

Willie offered to be his confessor, there and then. Willie also raised his hand and muttered absolution. But he found himself blessing Joe's hands as Joe had walked away.

Twenty

THERE WAS A considerable amount of celebration and public rejoicing in Umudiobia because of the news that the British had won in the North African war. And several stories were told about the victory. It was said, for example, that the British had sprayed the air around German ranks with some poison; and that the poison weakened the soldiers' bones, with the result that they could no longer pull the triggers of their guns. People drank in their homes and in public places. The Christians wore new or special dresses to church and they prayed fervently, thanking God that Hitler was no longer going to destroy the world. The band of Saint Barnabas Catholic School paraded the town in their new uniform of white jumpers with yellow, horizontal stripes; and they played their latest tunes. The pupils of the Anglican school staged a play called *War*, which tried to depict soldiers in action. They staged it publicly, in the market square, and attracted a very large and mixed audience, including Catholics and non-Christians. Indeed it seemed as if a common feeling of victory had removed, for once, all religious ill-feeling and differences among the people of Umudiobia.

Taking advantage of the situation, the Holy Spirituals made a public appearance, for the first time in many years.

Hitherto, the Spirituals had confined themselves, out of sheer prudence, within their compound which was situated at the extreme end of the town in the north. The stories told about the activities of Father George and his followers were enough to cause any small sect to disband. And the Anglicans, though not so ill-disposed, were sufficiently hostile. So the Holy Spirituals, to avoid any trouble, had kept strictly within their compound, and would not come out in the open to pray or to preach. And now, they decided that they could do so for once. But it turned out that the decision was a mistake.

It was to Joe that they went. The morning was bright. Anna had gone to the workshop, and Chinwe had also left. Joe was therefore alone in the house. But not for long, for he soon left to see the new building.

He had just got to the site. He saw in front of him a line of men and women all dressed in blood-red robes. They had small wooden crosses in their right hands, and a few of them wore small bells on their wrists. Silent and grave, they advanced.

About six yards away from the building, they halted and formed into a half circle. Then someone moved up from the rear and stood in front, facing the rest.

A crowd began to gather.

'What is it that they want?' Joe now asked.

'Let's wait and see with our two eyes,' replied some in the crowd, anxious not to miss the entertainment possibilities offered by the scene.

'Allelu—!' the leader intoned from his conspicuous position in front and held up the cross in his hand as if it was for auction.

'Alleluia!' they chorused.

'Joseph Okafo, we the Spiritual greet you.'

'We greet him.'

'Allelu—!'

'Alleluia.'

The crowd broke out, into laughter. Some urged the red robes to get on with the thing.

'What next?'

'A prayer.'

They collapsed on their knees, simultaneously, and held their crosses out.

'Jehovah on high, hear the voices of Thy slaves,' cried the leader harshly, shaking his unkempt head; and his left fingers began to play on the purple silk band round his waist. 'Let the Holy Spirit come upon him and his wife! Give them many, many children, please. Allelu—!

'Alleluia!'

More and more people continued to arrive. Among these were members of the two other churches. They watched peacefully. Some mocked of course, but only in low voices.

'Sing a holy song.'

They sang in praise of the Lord. They praised the good things in Creation—heaven and earth, land and water, sun and moon, man and woman. They clapped their hands and swayed their bodies; and they sweated.

'Rise up now and sing with all your strength!' he cried.

They stood up, spread out and continued to sing and to clap.

Then they began to dance. They danced to abandon and screamed. It was a mass orgasm, a terrible mixture of high-pitched emotions. Then, at the back, someone stole tom-tom beats into the confusion. Another started a metal triangle tinkling. Finally, rattles and clappers joined in. Staccato sounds mingled with red colour in a ghastly riot. And Apostle Dike, the leader, stood firm and undisturbed in front. From time to time he would call on Jehovah to hear the voices, thus adding more fuel into the conflagration. He would pitch his harsh voice over the noises and crane his neck as if he had just spotted uncooperative Jehovah at the back. The crowd simply stared, like people hypnotized.

'He has heard, Jehovah has!' he suddenly cried. And with that, the noises and dancing stopped abruptly, only to be succeeded by a big roar from the crowd.

'Allelu—!'

'Alleluia.'

'Our own church has nothing against any man who chooses to marry more than one wife.'

It was now that Joe fully realized what the visitation was up to. He shouted at them in anger. He threatened he would drive them away from the site if they did not go on their own accord, and at once. But the crowd intervened. Why should he deprive others of such entertainment? asked the crowd. He had better plug his ears if he didn't want to listen; or close his eyes if he didn't want to see; or both. But better still, he should go away.

Joe went. So did some others, mostly members of the Catholic Church.

'Did not the Holy Book ask us to increase and multiply?' went on the Apostle.

'It did, Apostle.'

'How many wives had the wisest man of ancient times?'

'A countless number, Apostle.'

The crowd murmured. The man must have been a very big chief, many said.

Then, the Spirituals turned and began to leave. Their leader, Apostle Dike, was convinced that they had made a very good impression on the people. He was convinced also that they would sooner or later achieve their aim, which was to get Joe to join their church. For otherwise, Joe would have objected to their visit in a more positive way. He was a future Spiritual, said the Apostle in his mind. There was no question about it. And he would be a very precious member indeed. . . .

They had gone only about three hundred yards from the site when a club struck the Apostle on the head.

'Chineke-e!' many exclaimed together. A few seconds later pieces of stone and dry red earth came flying from the bush on both sides of the road. Then the Spirituals, unmindful of their robes, invaded the bush. But the deep red easily gave them away to the enemy. However, they succeeded in apprehending four boys, two of whom were still armed with clubs.

That afternoon, they sent four of their members to Ossa to report to the Police. The four should tell the police that the Catholics in Umudiobia wanted to murder the Spirituals; that it was the Holy Spirit who had intervened and rescued His followers from the enemy.

*

Within a few hours the news had spread into most of Umubiobia. Several versions were made of it. Some people said it was the Spirituals that started it; that they had shouted abusive words on the Catholics. That was, of course, completely untrue; the worst thing any one of them did ever say that morning was that they were going to survive in the area in spite of Father George. Some said that the Spirituals were just passing when the Catholics ran out from the bush, clubbed them and folded them up in their voluminous robes. A few said that it was Joe that had invited them to pray for him so that he would have children.

Among these last few was the headmaster, Mr Akosa. And he said that out of pure malice.

Akosa had reason to bear malice against the man who was Anna's husband. He had failed to satisfy all the demands of his very important guest, the Agricultural

Superintendent. Because of that, the officer wrote a true and accurate report on the state of the school farm of which the headmaster was directly in charge and this year, for the first time in four years, failed to qualify for Teachers' First Class Certificate. That was in addition to the fact that he had attempted the London Matriculation twice now, without success! What was more, Akosa was recommended for immediate transfer to a smaller school. Already there was in him a noticeable change, for the worse. He looked sad and wasted. He took his cane everywhere he went and logged the boys more than ever before.

Akosa therefore held Anna and her husband responsible, and resolved to have his revenge before he left Umudiobia on transfer. The incident of the Holy Spirituals seemed to him to be the beginning of his opportunity.

He sent for Jerome at once.

*

Meanwhile the news had reached Anna at her workshop, but only the maliciously distorted version. 'What a shame!' people exclaimed. 'And he calls himself a member of our church. He waited until his wife would be out!'

She was terribly shocked, for she believed it was true. The logic was overwhelming. Joe had waited until she would be out of the house! That must be what he had had on his mind. No wonder the silence. If he didn't invite them, why didn't he dismiss them when they came? She had better go home. The shame was more than she could bear.

Some measure of reason came into her as she was hurrying home. She thought it could not be. . . . Then she thought it was true. . . . She thought it could not be. . . . It must be true.

There was nobody in the house when she arrived. She took out the duplicate key from her handbag and opened the entrance door. She stared, confused, at the floor, at the roof, and at the wall.

Soon, Joe came in. He greeted her, but Anna did not reply. Rather she asked sullenly:

'Have they left?'

'Who?'

'Those you invited to pray for you so that you'll have children.'

'Who are those?'

'You should know.' She paused. 'You waited until I would be away. Shame! See all the things people were telling me.'

'What devil has got into you this afternoon?'

'That's the way you speak, is it? All right, I'm a devil, I had better leave you alone to do whatever you please. . . . I had better do so.' But Joe had gone.

*

When Joe returned an hour later he found the entrance door open but no Anna. He sighed.

From the direction of Obieke's house, a woman's voice sounded: 'May thunder strike you dead, you evil thing that is called Obiakizu!'

'Why shouldn't it start with you?' answered the children of the neighbourhood.

He forced himself to laugh.

Twenty-one

OBIEKE said: 'We must summon our kinsmen at once and begin to look for her.'

'But why should she behave so unreasonably?' Joe objected.

'That question does not arise at the moment, brother. Our first task is to find her. We must make sure she's alive. She's a human being and not a fowl. Even when a fowl is missing people go out to look for it.'

*

Night had fallen. It was very dark, but the sky was clear and full of stars. Insects shrilled and flies flared. From time to time an owl hooted and announced the arrival of a kinsman.

Over twenty of them assembled in the sitting-room of Joe's house. A hurricane lamp was burning on the table. They began with funny stories and random discussions. They wanted to brighten the atmosphere in which they had found themselves.

'Do you know what?' someone said.

'Tell your brothers,' they replied together.

'I saw two men in the afternoon almost at the point of blows. Ask me what for?'

'Yes?'

'God.' When they had stopped laughing he went on: 'One belongs to Fada's church and the other to Siemes. The Siemes one said Fada's church and Opirichualusi are the same. That annoyed the Fada man.'

'He's a fool then,' Uzonda pronounced. 'Doesn't Opirichualusi look like the white man they call Fada? Only that Fada is white. Their dress is similar.'

'Did anyone see Jerome in the evening?' another asked.

'No. Why?'

'His eyes were red. I saw him hurrying to the church as if he was going to hang himself there.'

'It was the Opirichualusi affair that annoyed him.'

'The fool!'

'Of course he it is who owns the Fada church in this town.'

Joe came out from the bedroom and rejoined them.

'We were wondering, Joe, isn't it Jerome that takes all the money you people collect in the church?'

'What?' asked he absent-mindedly.

'He buys himself liver with it, now that he has laid off four of his five wives!'

'The younger ones at that,' said another.

'All because of the church!'

'Please may we go on to the matter that has brought us here this night,' Ikeli said.

They were all silent.

Then Joe related what had happened. He gave only the gist, with the result that he was through in a few minutes. When he had ended, some snapped their fingers, some sobbed, some groaned. Ikeli gnashed his teeth which, surprisingly, had remained intact. He was eating his sorrow in his heart.

'But I believe she must be alive,' Ikeli said. 'I believe she is safe too. What evil spirit is it that drove her into a thing like this? She's always been a sensible woman.' He paused, gnashed. 'But perhaps one can understand,' said he mysteriously. 'We—or rather you—all must begin at once to look for her, my brothers. I can't come with you. My limbs are weak and there's not much strength left in me.'

Without wasting further time, they agreed to go out and look for Anna that night. They grouped themselves in threes. They would first go to their respective houses and light tapers, and would then search until cockcrow. Everybody must return by then whatever might be the result. They would visit the daughters of the family; they would visit Chiaku; and they would visit the church women with whom Anna was known to be friendly.

As they were about to leave, Uzondu asked whether there was anyone among them who still wanted Uzondu, the son of Ayika, to marry a wife.

*

The cock had crowed for the second time and there was now a faint hint of dawn in the atmosphere. The kinsman reassembled. They were all tired and they looked like men at their wits' end.

Joe went into the bed-room. He brought a small bottle filled with tablets. He drank down two tablets with water.

'What's that for?' someone asked.

'For my head. It throbs,' he said.

Many stretched out their hands. He gave them two tablets each, until the bottle was empty. They swallowed without water. Uzondu, however, left his to dissolve in the mouth. Uzondu had refused to be persuaded that something drunk into the stomach could easily cure a pain up in the head.

'We'll go home now and have some rest,' one of them suggested. 'Let's reassemble later in the day—after the morning round of the palms.'

They accepted but prayed to Ojukwu of Umudiobia that they should have no cause to reassemble except to welcome Anna back.

When they had all left, Joe went in to sleep.

*

The sun was now clearly visible in the sky.

'Chinwe!' he shouted, and when she came he instructed: 'If anybody comes to look for me, tell him I've gone to the rubber plantation. Do you hear me?'

A feeling of anger had returned into him. 'She is most unreasonable. . . . Why should she go away?. . . . Where has she gone to. . . .' He spoke to nobody, and did not even respond to greetings on his way. He rode on mechanically, with an instinctive sense of direction.

It was nearly noon when he returned to the house. By then the kinsmen had already assembled again. They reprimanded him severely for his attitude to the whole thing. But he did not say a word. Joe just put the bicycle aside and flung the matchet away and began to wipe the sweat on his body. He cleaned his hand on his shorts. He then collapsed into an easy chair.

'What next?' Obieke asked, and he got no reply.

Then, outside the compound a bell rang—a prolonged, vibrating treble. Another rang.

'Who rings?' Joe inquired.

'Visitors,' someone answered outside.

He met them at the entrance. They were two. One was hefty and the other was smallish.

'Are you Joseph Ikafo?' asked the hefty one.

'Yes. What do you want?'

'It's you we want.'

'Who are you and from where?'

'We've come all the way from Ossa. It's the new District Clerk there that sent us.'

'You're Court Messengers then?'

'No,' said the man, smiling. 'Don't fear, we've not come on any tax raid. We are cyclists and the District Clerk has hired us for this trip. We've brought you a very important letter.' He began to open the bag which hung down from the bicycle frame. 'He says he returned from Ania early this morning and that he was given this letter to deliver to you.' He handed the letter over.

Joe read silently. He read it again. Then he read it aloud in vernacular for the benefit of the kinsmen. It said:

'Your wife is here. She arrived only a short while ago. One Willie Amanze of Umudiobia who says he is your cousin was arrested yesterday for sedition. His prospect of being a political convict may be said to be reasonably bright. That is what the Resident has said.

'I write in a hurry as the bearer, the new District Clerk for Ossa, is hurrying to catch the night lorry from Ania to Ossa. I have asked him to send special runners to Umudiobia immediately he gets to Ossa.'

It was signed Marius Ebe. Marius was the Resident's Clerk at Ania. He was also Anna's second cousin.

Twenty-two

ALL THESE DAYS Headmaster Akosa had been planning his revenge. And now, he was ready to act.

The day was Saturday, the same day, and the same hour, that the two cyclists from Ossa arrived at Joe's house. Akosa set out for Ossa to see Mr Una, the new police sergeant, his one-time school-friend.

He arrived at about seven in the evening but, when the light was very faint. He met the sergeant presiding over a bottle of gin.

'Please what can we do about this report which the Spirituals have made against our church?' he said, after some time.

'What do you mean?' the Sergeant asked.

'You're not going to take any action, I hope.'

'Well, that will depend on you.'

'If you are prepared to drop it my church members will appreciate it.'

Una laughed in a careless manner. Then he stretched out his both hands and shot out the ten fingers. Next, he lifted his feet and pointed at the toes. 'You see, don't you? Ha-ha-ha-ha!' he laughed again.

Then in reply, Akosa raised his right hand and displayed the fore and middle fingers, clenching the rest. 'Do please, close the case,' he pleaded.

Una frowned his face and shook his head.

They continued to bargain. In the end, they settled for five pounds.

There was in the sitting-room with them Una's third wife, Nwugo, whom he loved most and to whom he confided some of his secret. Akosa walked across to her. 'Cook good soup for my friend with this,' he said and delivered the amount, all in notes.

Nwugo exclaimed surprise. They exchanged confidential smiles; after which she took the money into her room.

'I can see your church members are more practical than those red animals,' Una now said. 'You people preach charity and you show it by deed. Ha-ha-ha-ha!'

Una drank more gin. 'Those idiots came here to report that your church members were out to murder them. No evidence whatsoever. And then, they went home and nobody saw them again. Perhaps they believe Mr Una is their slave.'

He left Ossa after breakfast the following day. He reached Umudiobia in the afternoon. After the evening prayers he summoned members of the church committee to his house.

He told them how he had gone to Ossa and was able to see the police sergeant in charge. He told them that he had already succeeded in persuading the sergeant not to take any action on the report which the Holy Spirituals had made. They all stared at him. Many of them stared gratefully, but there were others who stared with suspicion.

'It will cost us only twenty-five pounds.'

'What!' the suspicious exclaimed and some of them began to murmur.

'Well, it seems you are opposed to the idea of payment,' he said sternly, shouting. 'That's entirely your business: after all, I shall be leaving Umudiobia finally in a few days' time. But one thing is certain: if you won't pay the money, then you should expect the police here in a matter of two days. They will come to make arrests.' He spoke the last sentence brokenly, brandishing a finger at them.

Inspite of his attempt to brow-beat, there were still some to whom the whole thing was unacceptable. They were the younger ones. Why should the church spend money in that way—and so much? they grumbled. They would not subscribe to the idea. Let the police come instead; let them arrest the children who attacked the red-robes. And let them arrest the parents too.

Chairman Jerome felt that this was a dangerous argument. For it was the elder members who had despatched their sons on the holy war. He therefore overruled and ordered that the money must be paid, at once, through the headmaster. They would use part of the harvest funds for that. They still had fifty pounds unspent. The headmaster should leave for Ossa again the following day.

At that point Michael came out in open rebellion. 'Jerome, do you insist on using our precious money for an evil purpose?' Michael shouted.

Jerome's shock was so great that he could not even open his mouth. Nor did anybody else for some time.

'What is evil about it when we only want to save our church, rude man?' said Akosa at last. 'As for your savings, hasn't it occurred to you yet that the man who invited the Spirituals to pray for him should refund all the twenty-five pounds we gave to the police?'

That last suggestion heightened the disagreement and the meeting ended in confusion. However, Jerome had his way. He paid out the twenty-five pounds to Akosa. He also ruled that Joe should refund the amount.

Four days later, early in the morning, Akosa finally left for Ogolo, the land of breadfruit trees, after donating five shillings to the school and six to the church, for a last good impression.

*

Only a few hours after Akosa's departure from Umudiobia, Peter Imo came to see Joe in his house. Peter was an elderly churchwarden who did most things with remarkable efficiency. As a warden he had no parallel, either in the past or in the present. It was for this reason that he was usually stationed in the children's section of the church. Peter would crash through desks and bodies in order to reach a tittering child; then he would bring down his cane heavily on the child's head, after which he would twist the ear or the lips, or both; finally he would demand information about the mother's whereabouts in the church, and that in a tone which indicated he was anxious to treat her similarly. Most children knew him as Peter Dodge, from the fact that he dealt with noise-makers in the same way as the big, heavy Dodge lorry would deal with any who stood in its way.

Peter arrived at a time when Joe was about to leave for Ania. Partly because of this and partly because of the nature of his message, the reception he got was very much unlike what he was used to, as a messenger of the church.

'Look, I don't understand what you're talking about,' Joe said coldly. 'You'd better come again some other time. I'm in a hurry.'

'But that's a message from the church,' he warned.

'And so what?'

'Please give me the twenty-five pounds.'

Joe began to lock the doors. 'Let's go out,' said he some moments later. 'I want to lock the main door.'

'If you've no money now, you can let me keep your bicycle and some other valuable things until you're ready to redeem them.'

He smiled wryly. 'Get out! . . . One . . . two . . . three. Now—' His hands shot out.

Peter turned round and left the house, muttering something about rebellion against the church.

*

Joe rode the first six miles to Obizi. The sun had begun to set and no lorry was available; so he slept there for the night. Mid-morning on the following day he took a lorry to Ania, thirty miles off. The road was narrow with many sharp bends, and the lorry had long passed its peak form. By the time they got to Ania it was evening again.

He found nobody in, except a fat boy that looked as if he was Uzondu's son, and who did not seem to know his right from his left. He introduced himself as the husband of the guest from Umudiobia. In reply, the creature grinned and demanded to know his name and whether both his parents were born in Umudiobia or whether one was a native of Ania. He shouted angrily. That produced an immediate result; the boy ran over, across the road, to call Mamma and the guest.

They came in with Anna after some twenty minutes. But a few minutes later, Juliana, Marius Elbe's wife, left again.

'Everybody sends greetings,' Joe said.

'Including Adagu and her sisters, isn't it so?'

Some moments passed, then Joe told Anna:

'You look well here. It seems they are caring for you nicely.'

'Why not? After all, Marius is my own blood and I'm his responsibility.'

After five minutes Joe said to Anna:

'Have you seen Willie?'

He received a sharp no.

'I hear he's under arrest here in Ania?'

'So they say.' She walked out, and went to rejoin Juliana.

Joe did not speak to Anna again—not until after supper. Marius was back then. The four of them were in the sitting-room.

'Has your wife told you how she arrived?' Marius asked.

'Not yet,' replied Joe.

'You'd better tell him, Anna.'

She frowned instead and her lips became tighter still.

'No faces in my house, Sister,' Marius forbade, then proceeded to tell the story himself. A lorry met her a few miles from Umudiobia. She waved. The lorry stopped. She travelled in it to Ossa. Then at Ossa Anna found another lorry which was travelling to Ania. She arrived at dead of night. 'These women we marry can be very daring,' Marius added, expansively. 'More so when they want to defy us men anyway, that's what happened.'

He talked at length. He was a loquacious man, and he was pleasant too. He had one great fault however, which everyone knew. Marius would always insist on collecting his gift—raw cash, not livestock or foodstuff—before rendering official service. His nick-name was 'Missus-And-Her-Children'. That was because he was always telling the public that he was in duty bound to feed his missus and the children, which was impossible without money.

'And this my sister's state,' he said. 'Believe me, it has been causing me any amount of unhappiness. Since she arrived here Juliana and myself have been trying to persuade her to go to Enine hospital for treatment.'

'I've told you, I will not go there,' Anna declared emphatically.

'You will.'

'I will not. It's a C.M.S. hospital. I will not go there.'

'But we're not asking you to go and pray there, are we?'

'I don't want their medicine,' she grumbled.

'Well, it's up to you.' said Marius. 'As for me, I was brought up a Catholic but all churches are now one and the same, in that I don't go to any. Except on big occasions.' He guffawed, and his wife Juliana tried to rebuke him.

'I wouldn't like anybody to read the Bible over my head.' She gave a heavy wink.

'They can read it over your stomach if you prefer it so. But what do you say, Joe?'

'No objection,' Joe replied in an indifferent tone. 'But you know what the proverb says.' Anna watched from a corner and laughed in her heart. 'He who has been given a chase once by a white monster takes to his heels when green leaves begin to stir. We're just trying to come out of the present trouble which was brought about by the Holy Spirituals.' Then he said to Anna: 'I think you should go.'

'I won't,' she shouted.

'You will,' Juliana said.

'I won't,' she persisted.

'You will.'

'No.'

'You will. The hospital is wonderful,' Marius said.

'You will carry me there on your head, will you?'

'When are they going to try Willie?' Joe asked.

'It may not be long,' Marius replied. 'They've refused him bail.'

'Is he likely to go to jail?'

'I told you so in my letter. Anyway, we'll wait and see.

The wretched boy is still talking about liberation, even in the cell!'

'Does he still talk about Reverend Fathers?' Anna asked and turned interestedly.

'He's worse now. Yesterday when I saw him, he was telling the story of a certain Reverend Father who he says sends thousands of pounds every year to his wife and children at home.'

The wall clock clanked and strained, and began to strike.

'Quarter to ten. I must go to sleep,' Joe said.

'Why? You're not going home tomorrow, are you?'

'I would like to—if Anna is ready.'

'I'll show you the bed,' said Juliana and she walked up to him.

She began to lead him to the room.

'No, Anna won't go back with you,' Juliana whispered. 'I think I'll be able to persuade her to go to Enine hospital. Leave her here for some time.'

'I'll have no objection if she wants to stay for that,' he replied without interest.

Joe stayed for two more days in Ania. By the time he left on the third, Anna was sufficiently well-disposed to see him off. She also wished him a safe journey back to Umudiobia. And she asked him to greet Obieke and Obiakizu, and Uzondu, and everybody.

Twenty-Three

Back in Umudiobia Joe felt solitary and abandoned, because of Anna's absence. The hours dragged and the days were dreary. It had not been like that at the time he was angry, before he went to Ania to see her. Those days had, besides, been full of activity and there were really no lonely moments. Now that they had been reconciled, he longed for her presence and he felt awkward without her. This was especially so in the hours after supper—the time they usually sat and talked intimately and he told her his plans.

Wherever Joe went in Umudiobia people asked him about Anna. Not that they knew what had happened; they had only noticed that her workshop had remained closed for some time now. And besides, Anna had been missing in church and at women's meetings. Like the moon that shines at night, Anna did not have to announce her departure before it would be known.

More anxious for her return than any other, apart from Joe himself, was Obiakizu. Each day, mostly at meal times, Obiakizu would come over and inquire when she would be back. Obiakizu looked lean now; so he instructed Chinwe to give him lunch every day.

The apprentices came from time to time. They came in groups of three or four, not just in pairs.

'When is Mamma expected back?' they would ask.

'Soon,' he would reply.

'Oh, may she be back today! Was she well when you last saw her?'

'Very well indeed.'

'Will you be going to see her again soon?'

'Yes. But why do you ask?'

'So that we can send her our greetings.'

'I shall remember to greet her whenever I go there.'

'And tell her——' Then they would utter expressions of good-will and affection.

*

There had been a storm in the night, but at the approach of dawn it ceased. Yet at mid-morning the weather was still cold and chilly. The ground was sodden and the clouds were gloomy, and there was no trace of the sun in the sky.

Joe was alone in the house. He was cleaning his wrist watch, just killing time and waiting for the weather to brighten before he would leave for the rubber plantation. Three men came in. One of them was Peter Imo, alias Dodge. The other two were, like Peter, members of the church committee.

'We've been sent by the committee,' Peter declared in an impersonal tone of voice as soon as they had sat down.

Joe paused for a moment. 'Is anything wrong?'

'Well, it's the same matter that brought me here last time. It has now been decided—just this morning—that you should appear before the committee.'

'What for?'

'They will tell you when you get there.' Then one of the two others mercifully explained: 'There are three things. First, you invited the Spirituals to your house to pray for you. Second, you refused to refund the money which was paid to the police. Third, you forced a messenger of the church out of your house.'

Joe laughed. 'In that case, you had better go back and tell them I'm on my way already. Let them wait for me.'

'It's been fixed for next Sunday, after church.'

Joe bit his lower lip in self-control. 'I know it's Jerome who is pushing you old men into all this.'

'Into what?' Peter demanded; and he got no reply.

Bicycle bells began ringing outside the compound.

A few moments later four men came in, wheeling their bicycles. Still crossing the front yard, towards the house, one of them shouted:

'Are they here?'

'Who?' asked Joe.

'Peter and his friends.'

'You had better come in first.'

The four had now entered the house. 'If they've told you something already know that it is not our decision.'

'Shut up!' Peter ordered, leaping up from his seat, and his eyelids twitched.

'After I've said all I want to say.'

'You think you can handle us like small children in the church, do you?' another asked. 'Let me tell you, you old men in the committee must learn to respect your age. Joe, we do not want you to appear before anybody. We don't believe you committed any offence.'

They argued and quarrelled. They called names and pointed fingers. Their voices rose higher and higher.

Thus the discontent in the church community had crystallized into an open rift between the old and the young. The former, headed by Jerome, were the original, founder members, people who had made great sacrifices in joining the church. Some, like Jerome, had dismissed their wives; some had burnt the family idols and household gods in public; some had willingly given up their land to the church. Naturally, they expected to be obeyed in everything. They were noted for their orthodoxy and their fierce intolerance of other churches. On the other side were those aged from about forty downwards, who had been converted to Christianity at a later stage, and in their boyhood. They had not made great sacrifices; rather, they had been thrilled and lured by the prospect of adventure which the thing offered at the time. They were on the whole less zealous than the old ones and had a piously critical attitude towards the religion they professed. They also represented a new class of young men—traders and adventurers who had come to sudden wealth because of the war. Many of them were Oil Men—people who bought palm-oil from all the markets far and near and sold it at the Beach at Otta. The Oil Men were noted for their skill in cycling. They would each carry as many as six tins of palm-oil, one tin being of four-gallon capacity, to Otta, a distance of over twenty miles. Two tins they would sling down the bicycle frames; the remaining four they would tie inside a rectangular basket on the bicycle carriage. Because of their travels, they had come to acquire a broad outlook to life, and now they were willing to mix up with anybody, Christian or pagan, Catholic or Protestant or Spiritual. Inspired by Joe's success, these middle-age converts were prepared to adventure into an even wider world.

Indeed most of the older ones were very unhappy about this new class, the upstarts, that were upsetting the order of things. However, they thought the majority of the church were still on their side. To begin with, nearly all the women-folk, as conservative as ever, were angry with the young men for their impudence, for their showing disrespect to the elders. Then, the second generation Christians in the church, boys or girls, supported their fathers. But the strongest ally, potentially, the elders had was Father George. Everybody knew which side the priest would support if the thing should get to his ear. And probably it would. For everyone—young and old, Christian and pagan, Catholic, Anglican or Spiritual—was talking about the rift. The Anglicans were jeering at 'Father's children', forgetting that the same wind was blowing into their own camp, though not so violently. Only a few weeks before, some elderly members of the Anglican church had been accused of conspiring with the catechist, aged fifty and father of eight, to embezzle church funds. The accusation was yet to be examined, but some hot-heads in the church were threatening to take the matter to Court. The Spirituals, more solidly united now than perhaps ever before, mocked triumphantly. 'The Holy Spirit has struck the foe and set the members one against another,' they said in a newly composed song.

Jerome knew how laden the atmosphere was. Yet he called a meeting that morning to discuss what should be done to Joseph Okafo. Two of his friends, and his own appointees in the committee had advised him, privately, that the matter should be shelved. But he insisted. The meeting started at eight o'clock in the morning. Everyone of the eighteen members of the committee was there. The agenda was so vital.

It proved a very stormy meeting right from the start. The younger ones even threatened to depose Jerome from the position of chairman and to substitute him with Joe, the very man he sought to try. For over two hours they brawled, and they did not take a single decision. Then, Jerome ruled that Joseph Okafo must appear before the committee to answer to the three charges, and he got more than half the members on his side. He fixed the date and time for the next meeting, and for the trial; and then he sent out Peter Dodge and two others to Joe's house. But the other side had their own ideas. . . .

The seven quarrelled and quarrelled, and Joe just looked on. Even when they had left the house they went on shouting.

*

'I will catch you—even if you run into a lion's mouth!' Akueze shouted.

That was barely an hour after the visitors had left. Joe was sitting in the corridor. He sighed: 'This woman again!'

'And I must skin you alive today. Go on, I'm coming after you. . . . Yes, I thought so. . . . I knew you were running to that place. Go on, I'll catch you all the same . . . Evil One!'

A race for life knows no barriers or fatigue. Obiakizu ran very fast indeed and reached Joe's compound well ahead of his pursuer. He ran straight into Joe's arms, panting.

'What's wrong?' asked Joe. But Obiakizu had not recovered his breath yet.

'Villain of a child!' called Akueze from the door and began to step across the front yard. 'Let thunder strike you dead there. Or else, come and let's go home.'

'What's wrong, woman?'

'A whole coil of fish!' she gasped, then advanced, a big stick in her hand. 'That evil thing ate up all of it.'

'It's a lie,' Obiakizu said promptly, then turned his face away. Why should she make such mountain out of the mole-hill? He ate some fish—that was true; but it was a small quantity. Besides, he had gone about it diplomatically. He had sent Ijeoma who was Akueze's own child to bring the fish; and then, they had shared the thing equally. Akueze need not perhaps have known, for the quantity was small. It was Ijeoma who boasted virtuously, in her hearing, that she could be relied upon to keep secrets. 'For example,' Ijeoma had added, 'I didn't tell Mother about that fish, did I, Obiakizu?' That was how Akueze got to know.

'Did you eat the fish?' Joe asked.

He hesitated. 'Ijeoma gave it to me.'

'Don't call the innocent child's name again, you male-factor!' Akueze cried and lifted the stick. Obiakizu recoiled.

Joe's eyes glared furiously. 'What was it you wanted to do, Akueze?'

She did not reply. Rather, she lifted the stick again. 'Go away,' he said.

'Is that all you have to say about the matter?' she asked. 'Tell me, is that all?' She reached out her left hand, towards the boy, but Joe pushed her away. The stick in her hand dropped.

'Perhaps it's you who encouraged him to do it.'

'I've had enough of that. Go away now, please.' He stood up. 'Never come to my house again. You hear me, don't you?'

'I do.' She looked at him contemptuously and turned, and began to leave. 'You're very fond of children and yet you won't get your wife to produce for you. Castrated bull!'

Something surfaced from the depth of Joe's heart. It now ignited, exploded .... Someone rushed in, then out again.

Twenty-four

HE SAT on the bare floor, in the corridor of the house, and leaned with his back against the wall. His right leg was crossed over the left, his arms folded across his chest. He stared dumbly at the body that lay still on the ground, some yards away; and at the blood that trickled from the corner of the mouth. His mind had now begun to emerge from the buzzing and confusion.

The explosion had been terrific. It had transformed Joe— the tame, disciplined and reticent man—into a blood-thirsty lion. All the crude strength which he seemed to have laid aside, years back, were revived at that moment and charged into his big, hairy hands. His eyes had bulged and reddened, and rolled. His whole body had quivered, and the palpitations of his heart had reached his ears with a deafening echo, benumbing his senses all the more. Who had sent for the kinsmen, he did not know. He could not even tell when it was that they came in.

They were in two groups. One group stood behind him. The other surrounded Obieke who was some distance away. Only Ikeli, the old man of the family, stood over Akueze's body. Ikeli was examining the body and feeling it for the pulses, and gnashing his teeth.

'A man should eat his sorrow in his heart!' Ikeli sighed in tears.

'What is it you're doing?' the rest asked in rebuke. 'You should be advising us; instead, you're shedding tears yourself.'

His teeth creaked once more. 'My friend, Okafo, is that what has befallen your family?'

They joined again in reprimanding him—all of them with the exception of Joe and Obieke who still had not spoken. An old man, Ikeli had seen more in the situation than any of them. He groaned and gnashed and groaned and gnashed.

'Let's take the body inside the house,' someone suggested.

'No need. The weather is cold enough,' another replied.

'Not that. I'm thinking of people coming in.'

Ikeli felt the body once more. Still, she did not move. But the bleeding had begun to diminish, leaving a red patch on her cheek.

Joe stood up. A thought had come into his mind. 'Judge nobody; leave that to God.' That was what the priest used to say.

He went inside. He brought a cup of clean, clear water. He moved to the spot where the body lay. He raised the cup over her head.

'May I?'

'Go on!' they said, not understanding him fully.

On the swollen forehead he made the Sign of the Cross with the cup and poured the water at the same time, reciting: 'I baptize thee—Janet—in the name of the Father and of the Son and of the Holy Ghost.' He withdrew his hand abruptly in the end.

Her eyes opened, closed again.

'Did you see that?' someone exclaimed.

'Yes. She's beginning to come to,' another said.

They went closer. They thronged round the body. They asked him to repeat what he had said.

He went inside the house again.

This time, he brought a big bowl. He poured the water on her face and her chest.

She gave a shrill and feeble cry.

Their faces brightened a bit. 'She's coming round,' someone said. 'Let nobody touch her again, please.'

Then Obieke spoke: 'I think we should send for her people. Just in case—'

They sent Nwokeji and two others.

The three returned with Akueze's father, two brothers and an uncle. By then the scene had moved to Obieke's compound. Obiakizu had long been sent away to his grandmother's house which was a considerable distance off; and Akueze's own three daughters were in Nwokeji's house. A fat masquerade, hastily produced, kept watch at the entrance and sent away all visitors except those that were male and adult members of Udemezue's family. Obieke sat in his obi, his hands cupped behind his head. Akueze lay at the backyard of the dwelling house.

'Akueze, Akueze, Akueze!' called the father when he had seen the body. There was no answer. He shook it. 'Akueze, it's your father that calls you.'

Then her eyes flashed open and closed again. She mumbled: 'Yam and cocoyam are one and the same thing.'

'Akueze!'

Silence.

'See her head and see her body!' complained the younger brother. 'They've killed her.'

'Don't talk yet, Ekekwe,' the uncle said menacingly.

Soon they withdrew to one corner of the compound and conferred. Both the brothers suggested that they should go to Ossa on a hill to see the police. But the uncle objected. The police wore a double-edged knife, he said. Had they not heard of cases in which the police apprehended the very people that went to make a report? No, they should rather go in and demand from their in-laws an account of what had happened to their daughter and sister, he said to Akueze's father, his elder brother. And the latter agreed with him.

Back in the obi they were offered kola. By custom, kola should not be refused. So they accepted, and ate. After that, Akueze's father spoke.

'You sent for us, my in-law.' The tone was cool and seemingly dispassionate.

'Yes, we did,' replied Obieke wearily and paused. 'It's about your daughter and our wife.' He paused again. 'Something happened and she fainted. So I thought I should let you know.'

'Did she swallow a bone or what?'

'Not that.'

'Then tell us the full story.'

'Fortunately she's not dead,' Obieke tried to hedge.

'Dead?' interrupted the elder brother. 'As if we gave you a dead body when you brought coconut to our house!'

'Shut up, Anyake! Ehe-e, go on, my in-law.'

Obieke narrated in skeleton what they had been able to gather about the incident. After he had spoken, silence fell. Then Akueze's father said:

'I believe you're still speaking to your in-laws in riddles. Akueze told your brother that he had no child and then she collapsed on the ground and he poured water on her and she stirred. Is that what you want us to believe? But anyway, we've seen her and we've heard your voice. We'll go home first and narrate everything to our own kinsmen. May Akueze not die—that's all I can say at the moment. We'll go and see her again before we leave.'

He spoke with a gravity that mystified. Some felt the words had a veiled meaning. Others remarked that he had spoken very reasonably indeed. But of course he had always been a prudent, balanced man. How did he come to have such a bad daughter? Probably Akueze got her character from her mother who until she died was popularly known as Scorpion. What was the saying? It's the mother's milk that forms a child's character.

*

Days passed. Akueze's condition had not shown much improvement. She still talked incomprehensibly, and sometimes she would just stare into space wide-eyed. A cloud of fear hung over Udemezue's family. On the fifth day, they decided to look for a reputable doctor. And who could be more reputable than Emenike Nwoye of Ozala?

Emenike charged three pounds for the treatment. Half of that amount, he said, must be paid before he would even think of uprooting the shrubs or plucking the leaves. Joe paid. Joe promised too he would pay the remaining amount when it would fall due.

All over Umudiobia tongues wagged. Especially those of the women. The umuada would say:

'But he never seemed bothered all these years. How then could the woman's taunt have driven him to such rage?'

'The whole thing baffles your sister. But of course Akueze is an evil thing—there's no doubt about it. Like a dog that has some filth on its ear, she goes about looking for people whom to stain. But Ojukwu of Umudiobia will not allow her do it in Udemezue's family.'

'She may not die after all. Don't you know that the wicked don't die so easily?'

'I hear Anna is still not back.'

'Why? Let her stay where she is. She's of no use to us after all.'

'Perhaps our brother can now decide to marry another wife.'

'Marry? You will be disappointed, sister. I hear church men may re-marry only if the first wife is dead.'

Among Akueze's female relatives such converstion ran:

'He calls himself a man. Yo-o-oh! See how mercilessly he beat the small girl?'

'But who says he's a man? Let him prove to us through his wife.'

'Why didn't our brothers report the matter to the police at Ossa?'

'I'm told they will not unless Akueze dies, in which case the white man will remove him and cut off his head from his neck. . . .'

Some others said:

'Did you hear that Willie who is son of his father's brother, has been arrested at Ania?'

'Obieke's brother?'

'Yes.'

'The wretch! That serves him right.'

'Let him fight the white man there.'

'True. He can fell four hundred iroko trees in a single day with his mouth. Let him show us now what he can do with his hand.'

'Fight the white man! Stuttering, nothing else. Perhaps he has not heard about bombu—the thing which they say the white man drops from the sky.'

'Let the white man drop it on his head.'

'What is it a proverb says? "When you hold a small man by the two hands all his strength ends!" The white man has held Willie's two hands. Let him rule now and let's see.'

'Do you think Akueze will die?'

'I don't know. I hear though he smashed her skull and her bones.'

Whatever might be said in favour of the new way of doing things, others said, it lacked one thing: it did not attach sufficient importance to physical strength. Everybody knew that one of the surest and quickest means of establishing respectability in the land was still the use of the fists. Thus the unruly lad who threw others in wrestling, or who beat up his age-grade, was regarded as a hero, even by the very victims of his fists. People told all sorts of stories about Joe's hairy hands. Some nick-named him 'Hitler Hand'; some said he had iron inside his wrists. Even the church members were impressed. When he entered the church on the following Sunday, eyes watched him, mostly in fearful admiration. And nobody said anything, at least not to his hearing, about his case; or about the crisis in the committee.

Twenty-five

EMENIKE NWOYE, the doctor, ground some green leaves in mortar together with chips from the bark of a tree. He added a few drops of water and continued to grind. Then, after some time, he put down the pestle.

He smeared the slimy effect on Akueze's head and chest. Next, he rubbed some oily mixture into her nose. Akueze sneezed violently and her nose began to run. Finally, Emenike rubbed the mixture into her eyes. Moments later, tears flowed out and the sinister lustre in the eyes paled into light pink.

'She'll be all right,' he said, nodding confidently.

'We pray to Ojukwu of Umudiobia,' several voices said.

And really, she showed great improvement that day, and the next day. On the third day, Joe decided he could now visit Ania.

When he arrived he found only Marius Ebe's house-boy. Just like at the last visit, except that the boy looked less unintelligent today and was even prepared, in his enthusiasm, to open the master's bedroom for Joe. He actually turned the knob and pushed, but the door would not give. Both Master and Mamma were away at Enine, he said. They had gone to see Anna.

'How long has she been in the hospital?'

'Many days,' he replied. 'Let me see—Yes, ten days ago. No, it's nine. Yes, ten.'

'I see. Do you know when she'll be back?'

'I don't. Yes, Master says they may return with her today. Shall I cook for you?'

'Well, no. I had better go to the hospital first.'

Enine Hospital was exactly six miles away from Ania. It had been built by the Church Missionary Society of the Anglican Mission some seven years back. Without doubt, it was the most famous hospital within a radius of fifty miles. The building was not particularly attractive, but that was about the worst thing that could be said about it. Apart from that fact it was efficient in that which mattered most—which was curing the sick. The staff, from the white doctors down to the brown-clad labourers, were very kind and sympathetic to the patients, especially to the poorer ones. There was a story, believed to be true, that a patient once wept publicly just because she was discharged from the Enine Hospital and asked to return to her home.

It was therefore a surprise to Joe when on entering the ward he observed a general atmosphere of grief. The patients, all female, sat or lay silent. Some were mopping their eye-lids. One or two were crying, openly.

He saw Anna at the farther end of the open hall. With her were Marius and Juliana, his wife. Anna smiled very weakly and beckoned to him. He walked across.

'Anything wrong?'

She spoke in a whisper. A woman was in the labour ward behind. The woman had been screaming for hours; now she had no energy left in her to scream again. The doctor was already there; so also the matron, and some female nurses. What annoyed and distressed everybody most was the attitude of a certain female nurse, Anna added. The labour was just starting then and the woman was screaming intermittently. The nurse called upon her to close her mouth, and then added, to everybody's hearing: 'Ehe-e, you're crying now. Don't forget you felt very differently ten months ago!' They all burst out, shouting their protest and their curse. But the rude girl walked away smiling heartlessly. Since then, they had been upset by the insult to womanhood—and that from a woman-to-be. They intended to report the matter to the matron. They would wait until after the woman's case.

'Have you heard about Willie?' Marius asked.

'No. Please tell me,' Joe said anxiously.

'He's got what he wanted.'

'How?'

'He's now a political prisoner. The Magistrate gave him a year and six months.'

He snapped his finger. 'They haven't heard at home.'

'No. That was only yesterday.'

'How is Obieke?' Anna said.

'Very well. He sends greetings.'

'And Obiakizu, Uzondu and—who again?'

He hesitated. 'They are well. Only Akueze isn't.'

'The villain! What could be wrong with her?'

'I'll tell you later. You look well.'

'She does,' Marius said.

'The Sister says I'll be discharged today. Perhaps after they have finished with the woman.'

'Wait, wait, wait,' several voices shouted.

There was complete silence. One could have heard the the smack of lips opening for speech.

'Kia-a-ang!'

Then all the tension and all the suspense was dissolved in joy. The patients rose or turned in their beds. They shouted and glorified God for His kindness to a fellow woman. 'Enine, I believe in you,' they said. 'But how is the mother?'

The Matron came out soon after. Her face showed a big smile, which answered their question.

*

Supper was just over. Marius yawned and announced that he was tired; he then retired to sleep. Juliana said she had a headache. She retired into her bedroom. Thus Joe and Anna were alone in the sitting-room. As was their usual habit, they sat up till late in the night conversing.

She asked him about the new building, the rubber plantation, her apprentices, her sewing machine, and his trade in salt. Then she asked him to tell her more news about Umudiobia.

'There's plenty of it,' he said now. 'But first, tell me about the hospital.'

She tried to tell him what they did to her. They had put her in bed and sent her to sleep; and then, they did something, she didn't know what it was, to the inside of her body. She did not feel any pain. She did not even know that they had done anything to her—not until the nurses informed her the next morning. 'They are very kind people,' Anna said in the end. 'The whole lot of them. The nurses are wonderful—except that scoundrelly one. They treat you as if you were their own sister. The doctor is even better. Then the Matron!'

Joe laughed gently. 'I see you've now changed your opinion about the hospital.'

'Believe me, I didn't expect such treatment.'

'May be you will begin to go to their church when we get back.'

'Indeed!' Then she put it straight: 'It will never come to that.'

'Were there any Catholics there apart from you?'

'Yes; there were four of us.'

'And they didn't read the Bible over your head?'

Anna laughed. 'We made the Sign of the Cross each time they prayed.'

'They didn't object?'

'They didn't seem very happy about it at first, but we persisted until they got used to us. Then they began to make fun of us and we did the same about their own church. In the end, nobody bothered again.' She yawned. 'I must write to the Matron immediately we reach Umudiobia. She and I became very good friends.' She yawned again. 'Tell me, what do you say happened to Aueze?'

'You're yawning already. We had better keep it till morning.'

They were already on their way back to Umudiobia the next day before he told her.

Twenty-six

HE TOLD her the whole truth. She exclaimed at him and then, bending down, she shook her head and slapped her knees, in confusion. She looked up again, this time into his face, her countenance drawn.

'It was anger,' he said.

'I know. . . . Anger! . . . One day you will kill somebody with those hands of yours.'

He submitted to the rebuke. 'I was terribly provoked.'

By the time they reached home it was already evening. As soon as they had put down their things they went over to Obieke's house.

They found Akueze in the house with Ijeoma and the two other children. Apparently they had been conversing and telling some amusing stories, for the girls had been giggling, audibly, while their mother laughed aloud. But now, they all recoiled and became silent. Akueze sat up tense and fierce-looking, and the children spread out and surrounded her as if they were guarding her from danger.

'You look quite well today,' Joe said.

She smiled sardonically. 'Why not?' Then she pressed her left thumb gently behind the corner of her mouth where Emenike the doctor had applied a thick coat of brown, medicinal paste.

'I was so very sorry to hear about it,' Anna now said, in reply to which, she sighed.

Then, after an interval, Anna stepped forward, nearer to her. 'Akueze, ndo; biko ndo.'

Akueze's eyes flashed to the right and then to the left, as if she was summoning her three children to her aid. 'I am all right,' she replied.

Turning to the children, Joe asked ingratiatingly: 'So your father is not in?'

'No.' Ijeoma's voice was both harsh and abrupt.

'Where is he gone to?'

'We don't know.'

'When he comes in tell him I'm back.'

The girl merely nodded.

In spite of the cold reception, Anna felt relieved after the visit. She told him so as they were returning to their house. Akueze's condition was not as bad as she had feared, she said. Akueze seemed more irritable than sick. And when was it Akueze wasn't irritable?

*

Anna was glad to be back at her house. And Joe was happy at her return. Their company now had a fresh quality. They would not discuss the circumstances which had led to her departure—to her midday flight to Ania by the river. As the saying went, a good couple do not sit down to talk about past quarrels; they just forget.

Many visitors came. Some brought gifts. All welcomed Anna back after so many weeks' absence. But the kinsmen did so with some reservation. It would have been better perhaps if she had stayed on for some time, they felt. For they were still worried about Akueze's condition, about the possibility of her death and what that could imply.

The weeks passed. Anna had resumed her sewing and her

shed was again full to capacity. It was late October now—only some eight weeks to Christmas; there was a lot of work to do. To add to that, she had had much unfinished work awaiting her return. And she was determined to satisfy all her customers. Anna worked very hard indeed in those first few weeks. She would sew until the sun had begun to set; then back at the house, she would continue until supper time. She did not mind the strain. And she often sang with the machine.

Two things often disturbed her mind. The first was the rift in the church—the fact that Joe was the centre of it all. She had never liked the man Jerome, it was true; but Jerome was not the church. Anna did, in fact, advise Joe to pay the money, the twenty-five pounds, if that would bring the trouble to an end. She even offered to pay half the amount for him. Yet, he still refused. Then she offered to pay the whole. Smiling, Joe asked her to keep her money. 'I would never have believed you had up to twenty-five pennies,' he said, laughing. 'Don't pay for me. They will one day discover their folly.' And indeed, it was beginning to look as if the whole thing was going to peter out in the end. For the new headmaster, Mr Ukonu, was making serious efforts to heal the rift.

The second was of course Akueze's condition. True, it was not anything to cause serious alarm, but it was painful to think that Joe was the cause. Besides, Akueze's attitude to her had remained one of undisguised hostility. At times, when she visited her Akueze would wink heavily and turn her back. And she would always reject the gifts she took to her. It was all very disappointing, and one day she was constrained to speak to Obieke about it.

'I can understand your feelings about my wife,' Obieke had replied in his gentle and prudent way. 'You had better not bother again about gifts.'

It was from that day that she stopped bringing the gifts, although she continued to visit Akueze almost daily. Just as Joe did. Except that Joe usually went there first thing in the morning, before going to see the building under construction and the rubber plantation.

Joe had made that a habit now. Invariably, he would proceed to the building site straight from Obieke's house. He would tell her he went there to weed out the grass which had invaded the rooms, but in actual fact, he went mainly to admire the walls— the erect and sturdy stone walls which, as people of Umudiobia would often remark, were meant to defy weather and age, ram or axe. They were now at roof level, and the carpenters would soon start work. And then, from the building, he would move on to the plantation.

It was there, at the plantation, that he spent most of the time. The plants had been growing fast indeed. Many of the leaves had dropped at the onset of drought, and what remained had paled to light yellow; yet there was still much health in the young plants. Joe would walk from one plant to another, from one end of the plantation to another, cutting off the shrubs and creepers. By the time he returned to the house the shadow would begin to lengthen again.

But one day he returned much earlier. Anna had complained of a splitting head-ache and other things very early in the morning; that was why he returned so early.

'How do you feel now?' he asked.

'Well, somewhat better.' Anna contracted and shivered and yawned, feverishly. 'Did you see Nwokeji?'

'No. I've just come—straight from Akpaka.'

'He's been looking for you.'

'Anything wrong?'

She yawned again, and stretched. Then she wrapped the cloth more tightly round her body, from the neck down.

'I don't know. He wants you to come over to Obieke's house immediately you are back,' she said.

And then, a few seconds later, Nwokeji called from the entrance.

*

Emenike Nwoye, the doctor, had worked very hard indeed. Akueze had been able to move about and talk intelligibly. She only had occasional spasms. In the past twenty-four hours, however, her condition had deteriorated again. She would neither eat nor sleep. This morning she looked rather hopeless.

Shortly after Joe and Nwokeji had come in, Emenike Nwoye arrived. He examined her eyes, her ears, her lips, and her tongue; and he felt for her pulse. Then he said he would be back.

Anyake, Akueze's elder brother, arrived next.

'We must look for somebody else at once,' he said, surprisingly quite composed today. 'It's certain Emenike will not return.'

Without much discussion they agreed that they should look for another doctor. But who in the world could be better than Emenike? they wondered. Then Anyake suggested one Jacob Ikeogu, also of Ozala. Jacob was a very good doctor, he said. Jacob knew how to inject medicine into the veins so that it could come to immediate grips with the patient's disorder. He would go in person to persuade Jacob to come.

The sun had begun to set. Akueze sat leaning with her back against the wall, eating a meal—the first in nearly two days. Jacob walked in. He had a tarpaulin bag in his hand. He went and sat down close to her, then began to examine her body.

'Where does it pain you most?'

Akueze went on with her meal.

'Tell me.'

Anyake sighed: 'It was her husband's brother who ground her skull.'

'I've already learnt what happened,' Jacob said by way of a mild rebuke, then added profoundly: 'what you should never forget is that a bad word hurts the heart worse than ripe pepper does the eyes. She'll be all right, anyway, I think.'

Then he proceeded to announce the fee. Two pounds, he said, and before they could open their mouths he added: 'Not less a single penny.' Joe came forward and saved the situation for Obieke. Joe paid one pound before Jacob would open his bag.

'You're very lucky, friend, to have a brother like him.' Jacob remarked, and at the same time he put his hands inside the bag. 'Don't let this split the two of you. You've been very good brothers all these years, from what I've heard.'

Some sobbed, some sighed, while others groaned, in appreciation of these wise words.

'Is everybody here accounted for?'

'Yes,' Nwokeji replied. 'We're all kinsmen—except those who are our in-laws.'

'You will now hold her two hands for me.' He took out the loaded syringe from the bag. 'She'll have it under her neck.'

'Why not on her hip or arm? I've never seen it done under the neck,' Joe differed.

'No. It should be as close to the painful spot as possible.'

'I don't think it's ever given near the head.'

'You're teaching me my own work, are you?' Jacob objected, angrily now. 'If you don't want me to treat her I'll leave you people and go away. There are many other patients waiting for me in my house.' He made to put back the syringe inside the bag. But the rest pleaded. . . .

Akueze began to convulse immediately after. He told them it was nothing unusual. 'Her blood is absorbing the medicine,' he said. And they believed him.

The kinsmen discussed late in to the night. Then they sent four people, including Obieke, to Akueze's father's house. There it was agreed that the funeral should be held on the twenty-fourth day. In the meantime, the body was to be buried quietly inside the husband's compound. It was in the interest of both sides—the father and the husband— that the circumstances leading to her death should not be noised about. For it was Akueze's brother that had brought Jacob Ikeogu whose syringe was the immediate cause of her death. If the police should hear about it, they would look for the doctor and look for the man that had invited him.

Indeed Akueze's father would have liked the funeral to take place earlier so that the matter would be ended and the memory begin to fade. It was Joe's kinsmen who had asked for the postponement. They did that in order to allow Joe reasonable time to leave.

They all held that Akueze was not going to survive the pounding from Joe's hands. They also believed that Jacob, the doctor, had been despatched at the last moment by a sympathitic deity to remove the final blame from Joe. In matters of life and death, custom was inexorable and would always look for the primary cause. 'He that wounds a fellow citizen to death must flee the land.' It was stated clearly and nobody had ever doubted its meaning: nobody, Christian or non-Christian, had ever disobeyed or even tried to disobey. Joe must leave Umudiobia. And he must do so before the funeral, lest a vengeful spirit should direct a bullet to his body or to that that of Anna, his wife.

It was custom that demanded it, but it was also a matter of common sense. For how could he stay in the land to look at the cousin whose wife he had beaten to death? Obieke who had been very kind to him and extremely helpful! And with what eyes would he continue to see the children whom he had now rendered motherless? 'You it was who killed our mother—nobody else did.' That was what they would be saying to him in their hearts. It was perhaps more a matter of common sense than of custom.

*

Two days had passed and the body had been interred before he told her about it.

'Anna!' he began, his voice low and pathetic.

'Yes.'

He took a deep breath; then out. 'Things are going to be difficult for us.'

'What? How?' she demanded.

'Because of Akueze's death.'

'It's terrible,' Anna agreed without much thought. 'It could have been even worse,' she added, after some interval.

'Worse?'

'I mean if she had died as a result of ... It was that useless doctor that killed her. The one her own brother brought.'

He shook his head dully, incredulously. But she did not notice that. 'All the same, it's so terrible,' she said.

He began tearing at the hair of his head with his ten fingers. 'I started it,' he said. 'I'm the cause!'

'Joe!'

'Yes, I am ... And according to custom, I must flee the land.'

She moved nearer now and sat very close to him.

'What is it you're saying?'

'We must leave as soon as possible.'

She regarded him steadily while he kept on gazing at the roof, hands on the head, with the fingers interlocked.

'You're very upset?'

'I am. But only because of the circumstances under which we have to leave,' she said. 'How I wish it had not happened. . . . but as to our leaving Umudiobia, why should I be upset?'

His feet began to shake.

'Haven't we suffered enough here?' she continued. 'Remember all the things the umuada were saying about us?' Then her voice dropped. 'But I am grateful to God. He's always awake. . . . He alone knows when to give. . . But for Akueze's death! I wish she had lived. Ours would have been perfect joy.'

'What's all that?' he asked her.

'I don't think you have noticed?'

'What?' He sat up and set free his head, and kept his legs steady.

'That I am becoming two bodies.'

His eyes flashed. 'Anna!'

'Enine Hospital is wonderful. I didn't want to tell you more about the head-ache and other things until I was sure.'

He stood up, sat down again. Then, staring into space, he shrugged a number of times and his face brightened a bit. He was already going through the ironies in his mind.

And that was that. Ten days later, Joe and Anna left Umudiobia quietly for Obizi on the first stage of their journey back into a bigger world.